I0712725

ALL OF ME

SPECIAL 10 YEAR

ANNIVERSARY EDITION

HEATHERLY BELL

Published by Heatherly Bell Books

Edited by Katie Vorreiter

Cover by Elizabeth Mackey

Dear Reader,

Did I dream of writing a foreword to my book, ten years after its original publication? Not really.

All of Me is the first book in the Starlight Hill series, started in 2014 with the auspicious dreams of a fifty-something mother of three. My kids were in their teens and becoming young adults. I thought maybe it was finally time to indulge in a long held dream.

First, I sold a book to a small press publisher before a dear friend encouraged me to try self-publishing. The Starlight Hill series was born of my desire to write books set in an idyllic small town. These books taught me *how* to write.

Since then I've written numerous other books, and sold to a New York "big house" publisher. It's been a dream come true. Ten years flew by and now my children are adults. Somewhere in there, a few years ago, I became grandmother to a precocious little girl who owns my heart. And I have not missed a moment by taking time to pursue my own dreams.

If you're like me and you have a dream,

no matter what it may be, I encourage you to reach for it. It's **never** too late.

Thank you, dear reader, for taking this journey with me. And if you're new to my books, welcome to my little world.

I'm happy to have you here.

All my love,

Heatherly

xo

1

Not a good sign.

Instead of being ushered to HR to sign employee paperwork and W2 forms, Ivey Lancaster had been sent to the medical director's office.

Probably some minor mix-up with the paperwork. By now they'd received the glowing letter of reference from her mentor, Babs Holiday. Ivey was more than qualified for the midwife position at the new women's center.

Deep breath. *You've got this.*

Finally, Dr. Lillian Walker strode into her office.

"I apologize, but I'm running behind this

morning." She shook Ivey's hand. "We're on my son's third babysitter. He's four, and the master of his universe. In other words, he's going to grow up to be a surgeon." Lillian sat behind the futuristic-looking stainless steel desk, drew in a deep breath and leaned back in her chair.

Uh-oh. "Is something wrong?"

Lillian picked up a file, stared at it, and put it back down. "You could say that. This morning I found an orderly and a nurse in a closet, and they weren't looking for supplies. Dr. Harrison has taken an ill-timed vacation, since his wife threatened that if he didn't come along she'd go by herself and not come back. So I'm short staffed again. And then there's this desk. Who ever heard of a desk without drawers? It's beautiful, but why do I feel like I'm Uhura on Star Trek? I'd like to strangle the designer."

Ivey wished she could help, but she had her own problems. Aunt Lucy had a broken leg, and she'd be waiting at home right now. Wondering if her niece would get the job. So if Lillian could get on with it that would be nice.

"And then there's the women's center, and the midwife position." She scowled.

Directors scowling: another bad sign.

Ivey tensed at the overpowering scent of Lillian's lavender perfume, causing a sudden memory of Mom. On a good day, Mom had always been in Ivey's corner. On a bad day, Mom couldn't find the corner.

But this didn't make sense. Lillian had practically promised the job to Ivey, and she'd done well in all the interviews.

"It's not you," Lillian said.

Great. Could any good news start out that way? "So there's a problem."

"You guessed it. I've run into some objections from the obstetric doctors on staff." Lillian sighed and tapped a manicured nail on her desk.

This didn't come as any big surprise. Ivey had dealt with territorial doctors before, but Lillian had filled her mind with thoughts of a progressive hospital. "But you said ..."

"I know, and I'm sorry, Ivey, but I can't hire you. I can't hire anyone right now. The work requisition has been held up due to the doctors' objections. They went to the board.

Behind my back." Lillian's lips were a thin, straight line.

"I thought—"

"Think about what it's like for me as medical director of this hospital. The first female director. Our small hospital has been overwhelmed with budget cuts—"

"But this is why you would save money with the midwifery program. The hospital can save money when a midwife delivers a baby," Ivey said, but suddenly the problem dawned on her like a pink zebra in the room. Doctors, pressed between onerous HMOs breathing down their backs and struggling hospitals, felt their livelihoods threatened. She'd heard this story before.

"You can imagine how well it went over with the doctors on staff. I only have three of them on the L&D floor. It's hard enough to keep them here. Malpractice insurance costs, rising health care costs, and now the Affordable Health Care Act." Lillian waved a hand in the air.

Ivey sank in her seat. "I see." Until this moment she hadn't realized how much she wanted the job. She'd gotten used to being home again, among the hills and rambling vineyards of Starlight Hill in Napa Valley. Aunt Lucy constantly complained about its appalling lack of nightlife, but Ivey loved the quiet and the time to reflect. She'd been gone too long, kept away mostly by memories too tender to face even after all this time.

But she was back now, and that said something. It said Ivey Lancaster was ready to move on and make a life.

Now she'd have to find Plan B. Damn doctors. "Thank you for your time."

Ivey started to get up, but Lillian spoke again. "Unless, and I can't ask for this—" Lillian's steadfast brown eyes settled on Ivey.

"Unless what?"

"Unless you like a fight."

As it happened, Ivey had been fighting for one thing or another most of her life. Did she like a fight? Yes, but only if she could win.

"I like a fair fight. And I especially like to win." Might as well put it out there.

"I thought so. I'll be honest. I had a feeling it would be difficult to get this idea past the doctors. But it's time for some changes around here. And I saw something in you I didn't see in the other candidates. You don't give up easily, do you?"

A person with dyslexia didn't get through life without engaging in a metaphorical fight or two. Or three. "True."

"If you'll help me, I believe we could make this vision of ours a reality. Since the doctors' objections, the board has arranged for a subcommittee to oversee the decision. They've appointed one doctor to represent them, and I'd like to appoint you."

"*Me*?" She was a midwife, not a committee member.

Every time she'd had to make a presentation in school she'd clammed up. It had meant PowerPoint slides and reading out loud, and with her dyslexia, that was not a good time. She'd finally memorized every last word so that she wouldn't have to rely on any reading.

The whole idea was out of the question. "Sorry, I'm not a good speaker."

"You won't have to present. It's simply a written recommendation to the Board. What I need is someone who believes in my vision —someone who shares it with me."

"I see your point, but I'm not sure how I can help."

"I want our new women's center to eventually have a staff of midwives available. Women who have low-risk pregnancies deserve that choice, don't you agree?"

"Well, of course I agree." But that wasn't the point. The point was she wasn't going to be on any committee, sub- or otherwise.

"Thank you! You won't regret this. The doctors have appointed a first-year resident to the subcommittee. Some requirement by one of the benefactors. Don't ask me why, but surely the two of you can get along and come to some sort of compromise. You're both young, so you'll be flexible." Lillian stood up.

"But I—" Wait. When exactly had she agreed to do this?

"Follow me. I'll find the resident they've appointed, and maybe the two of you can arrange the first meeting."

She hadn't agreed to anything, and yet why were her feet following Lillian?

Lillian led her to a conference room and waved towards a chair. "I'll be right back once I find him. He's an ER resident, so if he's here at all, that's where he'll be. Sit tight."

Ivey didn't sit. She'd rather stand, thank you. Pace, more like it. She might pace her way right out of this conference room and right through the front doors of St. Vincent's Hospital. Hop in her SUV and drive back to the Vineyard Cottages where Aunt Lucy would be waiting.

But she did want this job, and the fact remained that a first-year resident wasn't going to be all that intimidating. No, she could handle him. Then the door opened, and Ivey's world shifted off its axis. She dropped into a chair before she fell down. This. Wasn't. Happening.

"What are *you* doing here?"

Jeff Garner should not have walked into the conference room like he had any business being here. He was supposed to be away in another state, completing his residency.

He met her eyes. "I was going to ask you the same thing. I'm here for a subcommittee meeting."

"That's not funny."

"Good, because I wasn't trying to be." Jeff took a seat on the other side of the table. As far away as he could get from her, because he was good at that. Interesting how some things never changed.

"Why aren't you in Maryland?"

"Because that would be a hell of a commute." He leaned back in his seat.

"Funny. So I guess you're no longer doing residency in Maryland."

Lillian breezed in. "Oh good, you've met. You two are the chosen subcommittee to meet and make a recommendation to the board on whether the women's center will add midwives to the staff."

Ivey stood. "Excuse me."

"Is there a problem?" Lillian turned to Ivey, eyebrows arched with the classic there-had-better-not-be-a-problem-because-I-trusted-you look of a superior.

Ivey glanced over at Jeff, who was smiling. *Yes, there's a problem. I didn't agree to this. Especially not with him.*

"Not at all." She couldn't give him the satisfaction of knowing he upset her that much.

"When do you need us to report back to you?" Jeff piped up.

"How about in one month? That should give you enough time. I'll give you two a few moments to get acquainted." Lillian left the room and shut the door behind her.

Get acquainted. That was a rich one. She was so well acquainted with her ex that she knew how many freckles he had on his back. And that would definitely not help her right now.

Jeff stared at his smart phone. "One month. That's doable. I'll give up sleeping."

Ivey snorted. She guessed she was supposed to feel sorry for him. Well she didn't. "This isn't going to happen. You and I can't work together. It's asking too much."

She thought she could see Jeff's jaw tighten, nearly imperceptibly. A chink in his armor. "I'm fine with it. We're both adults and professionals."

Except that right now she didn't feel much like an adult, because somehow Jeff made her feel like a sixteen-year-old again.

"You're right. If you can handle it, so can I."

"Good." His pager went off. He glanced at it and then stood. "Let's reconvene again tomorrow?"

"What time?" Ivey asked, as he moved towards the door.

"You pick the time. I pretty much live here."

"Okay. How about nine?"

"Fine." He walked out without a backwards glance.

Ivey swallowed. No big deal. She could handle this unfortunate turn of events.

But it didn't help that Jeff looked better, somehow, than she'd remembered. He'd grown into a man, cords of muscles in his forearms. Not tall and lanky anymore. Now his muscles had muscles. His dark brown hair was no longer long and unruly but closed cropped. Although some things never changed—he still had the same panty-melting gaze in his whiskey-brown eyes.

Those eyes had once regarded her with desire and tenderness, but now they only reminded her that they were virtually strangers. No matter. He might have a stare to melt glaciers in the Arctic, but it wasn't going to have any effect on her. She wouldn't let it.

2

———

Jeff ambled down the corridors of St. Vincent's, dodging orderlies and nurses on his way to the ER, acting like it was any other shift. Pretending he hadn't coaxed his heart back down into his chest cavity where it belonged. Asked it to please resume its regular rhythm.

He worked his ass off for this hospital, and when some lofty admin-higher-up had issued the command that he would represent the doctors on the subcommittee, he'd cringed and hoped for the best. Seemed to be all he did these days.

But then he'd walked into the room and seen Ivey, and just like that, it was five years ago again, and he'd come back home on break from medical school to find she'd left town to meet up with some idiot she met on a dating service.

He'd done his best to pretend that she wasn't even more beautiful than he remembered, and he had a pretty good memory. A sultry version of Snow White, with her espresso-colored hair and blue eyes. He found himself wondering if she'd wound up with the dating service guy. Maybe she'd married, and had kids with that loser. Kids that were supposed to be Jeff's.

Hopefully he wouldn't run into the man, because Jeff wasn't sure he could hold back the resentment he felt towards someone who had romanced his girl with a freaking computer while he'd been away at medical school.

Not that he should give a damn.

Dr. Stewart met him in the elevator, and hopped on at the last minute. "I heard you got put on the subcommittee."

"Don't know how that happened. I'd like to sleep sometime."

"Interesting. So you don't know. Well apparently one of the benefactors behind the women's center insisted that it be you. Why do you think that is?" Stewart eyed him with suspicion.

"Just lucky, I guess."

"I can count on you to let me know what kind of progress you're making?" Stewart was the head of obstetrics and had his own agenda when it came to the hiring of midwives on staff.

Come to think of it, they'd likely picked Jeff because he had no skin in the game. And that had been true until he'd seen Ivey. Now he didn't even know what to think. Probably because he'd been on his feet for twenty-four hours. Thinking had become difficult, and sleep a distant but fond memory. Fortunately his shift was at an end.

"I'll let you know." Jeff stepped off the elevator and onto the ER floor.

"There you are," Donna, the ER nurse, said. "I've got Frank in bay two."

He stopped moving, not an easy thing to do on the ER floor. "Again? That's the second time this week."

"You know Frank," Donna said from behind the nurse's desk. "You're his favorite.

But don't worry, Dr. Lewis has already seen him. Frank wants to say hi."

"After this, I'm going home. If I can remember where that is." Jeff made his way to the bay and opened the curtain. "Hello, Frank. What's it been, three days? You doing okay?"

"That depends on whether you think oxygen is a good or a bad thing." Frank sat up straighter on the cot.

"It's a good thing, and you know it." Jeff checked Frank's vital signs. As usual, Frank was the healthiest elderly man he'd seen in his ER. But the man insisted he had a heart problem and a breathing issue. And on Fridays, a skin condition.

"That's what I thought. So when I can't breathe, that's a problem."

"You breathe fine, and I think I've proven it." Jeff had tested his oxygen levels countless of times.

Frank coughed. "You should check my heart this time."

"What's wrong with your heart this week?" His vital signs showed a steady and regular heart rate, better than Jeff's had been a few minutes ago. The EKG looked good.

"I was sitting down watching cable television earlier, and suddenly my heart rate shot up into the stratosphere. I swear it must have been two hundred."

"Two hundred?" That would be a concern if it were true, but Frank's heart had never gone over ninety when he'd been in the ER. "What makes you think it was that much?"

"I don't know for sure, but when the young lady took her top off I remember thinking, 'For the love of Pete, those can't be real,' and that's when my heart started to gallop like a bunch of horses off to the races. The world is a strange place, Doc."

Jeff would have laughed, but he didn't have one in him today. "All right, Frank. Maybe stay away from the porn channels."

"You think that's it? Can I get a prescription?"

"You don't need a prescription, you need advice. Here, I'll write it on my pad if that makes you feel any better." He scribbled instructions to avoid porn, and tore it off. "Here you go. Have you seen your regular doctor? Last time you were here I asked you to make an appointment for follow-up."

"Nah, that doctor reminds me of a toddler. I'm afraid to let him touch me. Where did he get his diploma? The Romper Room?"

Jeff sighed. "Frank, there's only so much I can do for you here."

"You talk to me, and that's more than anyone else does."

Jeff faced Frank and used his official doctor voice. "Make an appointment with your regular doctor."

"All right, Doc. I'll try to get in to see him. But I'll be back if it doesn't work. Or if I get the rash back."

"And I'll probably be here."

"Right. Where else would you be?"

As he undressed in the locker room, he thought about the fact that Ivey knew where he'd originally been accepted for residency. But if she'd been keeping tabs on him—which he found . . . interesting—she'd missed an update on the past year.

When news got around to his family that he'd been recommended for a resident position at St. Vincent's, they'd waged a campaign for his return to Starlight Hill. Granted, he hadn't been back for much more than a short visit in the past few years, but his niece and nephew Becky and Liam were getting older, and his sister Ali wanted their only uncle around more often. Little did she know someone would have to be injured to see much of him.

He supposed it made sense that Ivey was back for a visit, but applying for this job meant she wanted to stay. Maybe things hadn't worked out with Computer Guy. Or maybe they'd worked out great, and for all he knew they'd moved their family to the best small town in Napa Valley to raise a family.

He didn't know and neither should he care. All he wanted now, besides a few hours of uninterrupted sleep, was to get through this punishing residency and secure his future. He hadn't been through eight years of school to give up now, even if at times he wondered if he was doing any good at all.

At St. Vincent's he'd become accustomed to the regulars, Frank being one of them. There was also the usual quirky small-town mix he'd come to expect——people he'd literally grown up around, like Ed, the accident-prone owner of the hardware store in town; the occasional migrant worker who'd met with the wrong end of a shovel; Marci, the hypochondriac; Eleanor, the pack-a-day smoker who insisted that he "do something" about her diabetes but refused to quit smoking or watch her diet; and the occasional wayward teen with alcohol poisoning.

Frank concerned him the most. It didn't take a psychiatric consult to see that the man was lonely. Jeff wasn't supposed to concern himself with how his patients did after they walked out the doors of the ER, once he'd pronounced they weren't in imminent danger of death. But he couldn't help being protective of Frank, who lived in assisted living and took too many trips to the ER.

Sooner or later, Jeff would need to get to the bottom of it.

IVEY UNLOCKED the door to Aunt Lucy's condo with shaking hands, closed it quickly, and leaned against it as though she could barricade herself inside from the rest of the world. The world in which Jeff lived in Starlight Hill again, breathing and eating and sleeping and Lord only knew what else.

And still looking too good.

One thought immediately sprung to mind: *I'm going to have to tell him.*

"What on earth?" Aunt Lucy stared from the couch where she lay splayed among magazine issues of *People*. "I saw a girl with the same expression you have on your face right now, but she was running through the woods from a madman who had an ax."

"I thought I told you not to watch those kinds of movies." Ivey walked to the TV and shut it off. She was the only one who could handle crime shows, and Aunt Lucy needed to stick to a steady diet of romantic comedies.

"Well thank goodness you're back. It itches again." Lucy shoved a pencil deep into the cast that covered her from knee to toe, thrust it up and down, grimaced for several seconds, and then sighed.

Ivey winced. "I don't think you should put a pencil down there."

"When you break your leg, you can talk. Lordy, when I get this cast off next week, I might kiss Dr. Stein."

"Please don't." Hadn't Ivey endured enough embarrassment when Lucy asked the doctor how a woman could have sex with a cast on her leg, and if he could recommend what position might work best?

"I'm kidding. He's not my type."

Not at all. Unfortunately he was at least thirty years older than her type, which lately tended towards thirty-something unemployed men. Not a bad thing, except for the fact that her aunt was fifty-eight.

The problem was that Aunt Lucy's priorities had changed when she'd won the California lottery ten years ago, and now she seemed determined to suck the marrow right out of life.

When she'd phoned about the broken leg she'd suffered skiing in Vail on the constant vacation she called her life, Ivey rushed back from Los Angeles to help. Aunt Lucy had once helped Ivey during a difficult time, and at least now she could pay back her kindness by tending to her every need. Even if every one of those needs was getting on Ivey's last nerve.

"How did it go at the hospital? Did you get the job?"

"No. I've been put on a subcommittee with one other doctor. Together we're supposed to come up with a recommendation for the board next month." Ivey grabbed a soda from the fridge and held it for a second against her flushed cheeks. Then she plopped down on the couch next to Lucy.

"A recommendation for what?"

"Whether they should even hire midwives for the women's center. I guess some of the doctors have objections."

"Oh they do, do they? Well la-di-da. So who is this doctor you're going to be working with?"

"Jeff Garner," Ivey said flatly, hoping she'd successfully removed every ounce of emotion from her voice.

Aunt Lucy's eyebrows went up to her forehead, and that was hard to do with all the Botox. "Oh. Oh, dear."

"Yeah."

Aunt Lucy fanned herself with the latest edition of her movie star magazine, and a picture of a smiling Brad Pitt and his arsenal of children waved in Ivey's direction. "It's for the best. Time you told him everything."

"No! It's not."

"He has a right to know." Aunt Lucy had

always believed that, but she'd supported Ivey's decision.

"What do you think I should tell him? Hey, Jeff, five years ago when I left town I was pregnant with your baby. Thought you should know. So have a great day."

"I never said it would be easy."

"I don't need to make enemies at the hospital, and he'll hate me."

"Or it will finally make sense to him that you took up with someone on the Internet and left town like you had something to hide. I wish you'd come up with a better story than that one. Everyone in town talked about you for weeks. Took sides and made me crazy. What a ditzy move that was."

Ivey threw her hands up in the air. "Why is it so crazy to believe I met someone on an online dating service? Hundreds of millions of people have found love there, or so the commercials say. And that's where I met Joe."

"Joe? I thought the name you made up was John."

"Don't you think I can remember the name of my own fake boyfriend? It was Joe. I've always liked that name. Joe's always a good guy. You can count on Joe."

Aunt Lucy shook her head. "You better make sure you keep that name straight if you want to keep up this ruse."

"I don't need to talk about Fake Joe. It didn't work out."

"If Jeff's like most men, the last thing he'll want to do is talk about your ex-boyfriends. Fake or otherwise."

"I'm not going to talk to him."

"How will you communicate? Sign language?"

"No. I'm going to get off this subcommittee." Ivey stretched her legs out on the couch. "It's the only way, so that's what I'm going to do."

No way would Lillian make her do this. She'd be there bright and early tomorrow morning and explain everything. Maybe even throw in a little tear or two. Those weren't all that hard to call up when she thought about the past and how badly she'd screwed everything up.

"I don't think that's a good idea. If you want this job, fight for it. Don't let him chase you out of town again."

"He didn't chase me out of town. I went willingly."

"Because you didn't want to be a glitch in his schedule. Well, Missy, it took two to make that baby."

"You don't have to tell me that." As it so happened, she had a distinct memory of the event, and she definitely hadn't been alone. Not that she wanted that image in her head right now.

But Aunt Lucy did have a point. She wasn't going to go anywhere, not this time. If it would be difficult for Jeff to have her stay in town, too bad. She was not going to accommodate him anymore.

"I want the job. It's not that. I only want off the subcommittee."

"Fine. But what's he going to think about that?"

"You know what? I don't care."

With a little more effort, Ivey might be able to convince herself of that.

3

Eight hours of fitful sleep were not enough, especially when Ivey had invaded half of Jeff's dreams, but they'd have to do.

Still, when he opened the door to the conference room at precisely nine o'clock the next morning, he'd half convinced himself that yesterday had been a nightmare. He wasn't really going to be on this subcommittee with his ex-girlfriend-slash-first-love.

But no, she was here. Not a figment of his imagination. He rubbed an eye with the back of his hand, more exhausted than disbelieving.

"What's the matter? Didn't sleep well last

night?" Ivey looked up at him from her seat at the long conference table.

"Something like that."

"None of this bothers me, in case you were wondering. I slept like a baby."

"You always did. More like the dead, actually." He took a seat. "You shouldn't see me as the enemy. I'm the sucker that got appointed to this. I honestly don't care what happens with the women's center. They could hire a fleet of clowns and I wouldn't care."

Ivey eyed him with the Death Stare. "Are you comparing midwives to clowns?"

Yeah. He should have thought that off-the-cuff comment through a bit better. Blame it on the lack of caffeine, because there wasn't enough in the state to keep him firing on all cylinders.

"No. I've always liked clowns." Sue him. He couldn't resist.

Ivey stood. Today she wore a white ruffled top that went up to her neck, and her long hair in a tight bun. If it wasn't for the pencil skirt, she'd look like a prairie woman. And what was up with that?

"Let's go."

"Where are we going?"

"We're going to talk to Lillian. I'm going to tell her I can't do this, and I want you there when I do it."

"What can I say? I'm honored." He held the door open, and followed her out, trying like hell not to check out her ass while he did. Epic fail. Dammit, even dressed like Dr. Quinn Medicine Woman she managed to arouse him.

Which would mean he'd stepped into a time machine, because that shouldn't be happening.

Usually the hospital smelled like antiseptic and on a bad day in the ER like blood, but at the moment all he could smell was Ivey. Standing near her in the elevator, he swore he could smell the soft scent of vanilla. Did she still wear the same body spray he'd bought her years ago? The one that tasted as good on her as it smelled?

"It doesn't have to be like this," he finally said after a few more minutes of silence. Maybe they could at least put up the appearance of friendship.

Her shoulders seemed to relax an inch or two below her ears, but then she looked at the floor. "You were supposed to be in Maryland."

"Sorry to disappoint you."

"I didn't mean—" She stopped midsentence. "Look, my Aunt had an accident and she needed me. I didn't know you were in town. Then this opportunity came up."

"You should take it if that's what you want. Couples break up all the time, and it doesn't mean one of them has to leave town. That was your choice."

She seemed to swallow hard at that. "I'm aware of that."

The elevators doors swung open, and Ivey continued walking towards Lillian's office, so he followed. If she wanted off this committee, they'd probably appoint someone else. Meanwhile he'd be stuck with the responsibility. Hopefully the new subcommittee member would be a man. Or ugly.

Ivey knocked once on Lillian's door, then hesitated and knocked again.

Lillian opened the door, tissue in hand. "Come on in."

It appeared that the medical director had been crying. Her eyes were red and her cheeks blotchy. But that couldn't be, because there was no crying in medicine. Only patients were allowed to cry. Sometimes.

So far this day was not shaping up to be any better than the last forty-eight hours.

"Is everything okay?" Ivey asked.

"Wonderful. I just have something in my eye. I'll need to find a new babysitter though. My son hid the babysitter's dentures. I could barely understand the woman when she called to quit on me. This is the third babysitter we've been through. Did I mention that? But you don't need to hear my problems. What can I do for you?" Lillian sniffed into her tissue and offered them a brave smile.

Jeff turned to Ivey and didn't say a word. It was for the best that he remain mute.

"I wanted to tell you that—" Ivey began and then stopped. Glanced at him.

For help? Really?

"Yes? What is it?"

Ivey let out a breath. "I'm going to enjoy working with Dr. Garner. I think we'll make a good team."

The director sighed deeply. "That's what

I like to hear. Finally some good news. You've made my day."

On the way back down in the elevator, Ivey pointed a finger in his direction. "Not a word. It's hard for a working mother to find good child care. Besides, we can make this work, can't we? If we sit on opposite sides of the table and divide up the work."

Funny how Ivey behaved, when she'd been the one to leave him. Suddenly he'd had enough of her games. "Explain why you're so pissed when you're the one who broke up with me."

"That's good, Jeff. Are we now going to rewrite history? Let's go ahead and get rid of the Vietnam War while we're at it. *You* broke up with *me*."

"Speaking of rewriting history, you just did that." He stepped off the elevator and walked briskly ahead of her to the confer-ence room.

He opened the door and stood aside for her. Ivey started to walk through, then stopped. She took a deep breath and then gave him a long look with those blue eyes that sometimes looked violet, depending on the light. "Before we walk in there, we have to agree to leave our personal lives outside. That's the only way I'll do this."

"You got it."

"Good." Ivey walked to the conference table and opened her tablet. "Let's get started."

Jeff went ahead and pretended that magical pixy dust had settled over them the moment they crossed the threshold. For the next two hours, they talked birth statistics, labor and delivery, and emergency C-sections. Ivey's cheeks got a little pink every time they discussed a woman's pregnancy and risk factors, a bit strange for someone who claimed to be a midwife.

"I'm sure your part in all of this is to sway the board that it might be best to keep midwives out of a hospital," Ivey said, tapping away furiously on her tablet.

"Wrong again." He leaned back. "My part in all of this is to remain objective and give an honest recommendation."

And he would try like hell to remain objective, even if all he wanted to do was take her home and show her how much he'd missed her. Then do it all over again.

She arched a brow. "And you think you can do that?"

Maybe. Probably. Oh hell. No. "What part of 'I'm not the enemy' do you not understand?"

Ivey shook her head. "Sorry."

"Dr. Allen Stewart." She should know the name of her real enemy, and it wasn't Jeff.

"Who?"

"He thinks the hiring of one midwife is the beginning of a long, slippery slope in which he ends up destitute on the side of the road."

"He's not any different than most doctors I've known."

"How long have you been a midwife?" He changed the subject, hoping she wouldn't notice he'd taken a tangent leading toward the personal. In the past, biology had never been her strong suit, unless you counted the time they'd spent in the bedroom.

"I worked as an apprentice midwife for Babs Holiday, and for the last two years I've been on my own."

"Why not work as a home birth midwife?"

"I want to work in a hospital. We need to

stop acting like doctors and midwives are mortal enemies and learn to work together."

"It's not going to be easy. And Stewart is a hard-ass."

"So you don't think I can handle him?"

"I didn't say that." Jeff didn't like this little semi-friendly exchange. It was easier to keep the emotions bottled up and tamped down tight where they couldn't bother him. Right now they were rising to the surface and annoying the hell out of him.

Just because he was lonely and couldn't remember the last time he'd been laid, it was no reason to take up with the ex.

Ivey shut her tablet. "Why don't we end for today?"

"Good idea. My shift starts in an hour, so I'm going to grab lunch."

"Another long shift?"

"Yep."

Right about now, Ivey would be counting her blessings that she hadn't wound up with him. Maybe whoever she'd wound up with could give her more than two hours a day of his time. "At least you'll know where to find me."

"Right." Ivey glanced up at him, the hint

of a smile on her lips. "Will you be in the cafeteria? I mean, in case I need you. To ask you a question."

"No, I won't be in the cafeteria because that would be crazy."

He'd be heading to Em's. She made the most succulent pot roast he'd ever tasted, and he'd grown accustomed to the fact that a home-cooked meal waited for him every night he could make it to her kitchen before closing time. Even though there hadn't been many of those nights lately.

"That bad, huh?"

He hesitated for a second, and then hormones won the day. Again. "You should come with me. I'll show you the best place in town to eat."

Her forehead wrinkled. "No, that's all right."

"What's the big deal? We could catch up. Since we can't speak about anything personal when we cross the threshold."

Damn, he hated the fact that he wanted to be with her even for a few more minutes. Maybe some place where she'd loosen up a bit. This whole prairie woman look wasn't the Ivey he remembered.

She clutched her tablet. "Why do we have to talk about anything personal?"

"We don't. But we were friends first, and if nothing else we could be that again." What the hell was wrong with him? This was Ivey. Ivey who left him right at the toughest time of his life. He should be pissed.

Except for the fact that what she'd said earlier had brought back an old memory he'd long buried. First year of med school he'd been drowning. He knew the stats for first year students. So did Ivey. The dropout rates were astronomical, and he couldn't join those ranks. Not with how much his middle-class parents had sacrificed to help put him there. He and Ivey had managed a long-distance relationship for four years of pre-med, but that first year of med school she'd become unbearably clingy and needy.

So yeah, he'd told her he wanted a break. He hadn't expected she'd listen so well. Interesting how he'd rewritten that in his mind, mostly because from the time she'd been sixteen Ivey had always been his, and he'd never expected that to change. He'd thought she might back off and let him breathe a bit. Let him come back to her, because he always would.

Hadn't quite worked out that way.

"Friends? You and me?" Ivey asked.

Why the hell not? Stranger things had happened. He'd seen them firsthand in his ER.

IVEY AND JEFF could not be buddies.

On the other hand, he was the only other member on the subcommittee, and he could exert a deep influence on the other doctors. Someone had put him there because they trusted his judgment. And if she wanted this to go well, it would be important to have Jeff on her side.

Like old times.

And he had asked her out to lunch. Not a date, just friends. He wanted to show her a decent place to eat near the hospital. Something he'd do for any colleague.

"Well, what do you say?" He was still waiting for an answer.

"All right," she said, because she'd always had impulse control problems around him.

She hadn't known what to expect, but it wasn't to walk. Still, she slipped her tablet in her bag and followed Jeff's long strides. Across the street from the hospital and two blocks to the east stood a little diner Ivey remembered all too well.

"Mama's Kitchen? I remember this place," she said as he held open the door to the diner.

"Under new ownership. I heard that Em and her husband Si took over about three years ago. I'm a regular."

Good thing the place was under new ownership because the old owner, Mr. Peterson, was a sixty-year-old man who hated kids. He'd inherited the place from his mother, the original Mama. The man hated teenagers in particular, and when she and Jeff used to come in here and sit at the booth in the corner, he would yell, "Let me see some daylight between you two!"

The aromatic smell of coffee, sizzling bacon, and burgers permeated the diner. No doubt about it, this place smelled like a mother's kitchen should, as long as the mother didn't care about cholesterol and calories.

"Hey, Si, would you look who's here." The woman who greeted them had short salt-and-pepper hair and earnest blue eyes.

A ponytailed man Ivey assumed was Si ducked his head through the kitchen partition, bumped it, and rubbed his forehead. "Damn this thing. What did you say?"

"I said your favorite doctor is here," Em shouted back at his puzzled look, then waved him off. "Never mind. He can't hear me back there."

They followed Em to a booth, and before they sat down, Jeff introduced Ivey. "She used to come here also."

"Ah." Em leaned down and rubbed Ivey's shoulder. "Don't worry, dear. That blue ribbon is long since gone. You'll find I'm apolitical in every way. I love everyone as long as they eat."

When Em walked away, Ivey couldn't help but ask. "What blue ribbon?"

The menu suddenly seemed of deep interest to Jeff, a man who by his account should have it memorized. "After we broke up, some of the business people in town took sides. Those who liked me hung blue ribbons in their establishment. Those who liked you put up pink ones."

He looked so serious, and that's what kept her from laughing. "Is that supposed to be a joke? I'd forgotten about your weird sense of humor."

He continued reading the menu as if it were a medical journal. "Mr. Peterson put up a blue ribbon, but that was before Em bought the place. She took it down."

"Aunt Lucy mentioned something about people taking sides, but I thought she was exaggerating as usual." Blue and pink ribbons? Had the whole town gone mad together?

"How many pink ribbons were there?" It would be nice to know who her real friends were.

He met her eyes. "I didn't count. I thought it was as ridiculous as you do."

"But Mr. Peterson had a blue ribbon. He always liked you better."

"You were the one who used to practically sit in my lap every time we were here."

Ivey felt flushed at hearing the truth stated so matter-of-factly. Even if Jeff had never protested the seating arrangements. "Mr. Peterson was a misogynist."

"Everyone's over it now. But I wouldn't go into the hardware store on Main Street."

Ivey let out a deep sigh. Everyone had held it against her for leaving town for a man she met online, but it had turned out to be the best place to find a fake boyfriend.

Em came and took their orders. Without the menu, Jeff turned his full attention on Ivey. "So how's lover boy? John, was it?"

"Joe." Why couldn't anyone get his name right? Even imaginary fictional characters deserved a little respect.

"Are you sure?" Jeff narrowed his eyes. "I'm pretty sure it was John."

"Thanks, but I think I know the name of my ex-boyfriend better than you do."

"Ex?"

Ivey played with the edge of her napkin. "It didn't work out. Next subject."

Why had she ever agreed to leave the sanctuary of the conference room where they'd agreed not to discuss personal stuff? It was a trick, and she should have seen it coming. Damn Jeff and his perfect build, smoldering eyes, and aesthetically pleasing jawline. If he didn't stop talking about the past, she might be rearranging that perfect face so that he would need to see one of his colleagues for a little rhinoplasty.

Em brought out their burgers and sweet-potato fries. They'd both ordered the same thing.

"How are your parents? And your sister?" If he wanted to talk personal, two could play this game.

"My parents moved to Oregon a couple of years ago. They come down every year for the Grape Festival. Ali lives in town with her husband Bob and two kids."

"Two?"

"Becky is four and Liam is two."

Ivey took a gulp of water and swallowed hard. She should have never opened up this line of discussion. "So what about your love life?"

He gave her a long look. "What love life?"

"You asked about mine."

"I don't have one. The hospital is my sig-nificant other."

"Ah, the life of a resident."

"Only the highly tolerant need apply."

While it was difficult to believe that

someone who looked like Jeff didn't have the nurses in a tizzy every day, it was possible that he'd try to keep his personal life and business separate. Though not likely.

"So what happens if the board decides against hiring a staff of midwives?" Jeff asked between bites.

"You mean after our subcommittee's powerful recommendation that they do?"

He grinned and bit off a french fry. "Of course."

"I suppose I don't get the job."

"And then what?"

She hadn't thought that far ahead, having always been a fly-by-the-seat-of-her-pants type. But she wanted to stay, despite the news of the pink versus blue ribbons. Maybe she'd find out who'd had a pink ribbon displayed and thank them for their support.

"I'll find another job."

"You won't leave town again?"

"I won't. Why would I?"

"I don't know. You have a history of leaving when you don't get your way. I break up with you, and you leave town."

"Oh so you admit it now."

"I remember saying I needed a break. I was trying to get through the first year of medical school. But I was already out of state, so I don't see why you had to leave."

Because then everyone would have seen her pregnant body, and in this town of blue and pink ribbons Jeff would have found out. The first person to see her throw up would have phoned him and probably given details as to where she'd been and what she'd eaten before she threw up.

"The reason I left town was because Joe was in LA, and long distance relationships don't work."

Jeff leaned back in his seat. "You mean John."

Ivey resisted the urge to pound his gorgeous face and hit the table instead. "Joe, dammit."

Jeff grinned. Fine, she'd let him have his fun. She still needed him to be on her side.

"We managed to have a long distance relationship."

"And look how well that worked out." Ivey picked up a french fry.

Jeff had a funny look on his face, his eyebrows arched and a smile tugged at the corners of his mouth.

"What's so funny?" That's when she realized she'd reached for a fry off of his plate instead of her own. Ack. She dropped the fry and drew back her hand like a snake had bit it.

"That's all right. You can have my fries." He pushed the plate in her direction. "Force of habit. The last time you and I ate together we...shared more than fries." He gave her a wicked grin.

She pushed the plate back. "I don't want your stupid fries."

"C'mon Ivey, you know you want some." He pushed it back in her direction.

She didn't like that penetrating look in his eyes. The air between them charged and electrified. The overwhelming knowledge that despite everything, they weren't quite done with each other.

But they had to be. Ivey pushed the plate back. "That's where you're wrong. I'm done."

And she had to remember that.

4

———————

One week later, Ivey had quizzed Aunt Lucy thoroughly and found that the fabric store and the hair salon Lucy used to run both had pink ribbons displayed proudly for a time. Even the bookmobile (Ivey was a regular) had a pink ribbon. The vintners had fought hard to stay out of it.

Somehow Ivey recovered from the french-fry stealing incident in which her hand had subconsciously gone where it shouldn't have. She couldn't have that happen again. Couldn't have her hand touch that gorgeous head of thick brown hair, or let it graze the stubbly jawline. No. Couldn't have that.

Aunt Lucy's screechy voice pulled Ivey from her thoughts. They were at the doctor's office, and Lucy's cast had been removed.

"Six long weeks! You have no idea how difficult this has been for me. I haven't gone this long without sex since—well, I can't remember when."

While Ivey prayed the ground would open up and swallow her whole, Dr. Stein ignored the comment and continued to examine Lucy's x-ray. "The bone healed nicely. You're quite lucky. We can't always expect that in a woman of your age."

Ivey sucked in a breath. *Oh no, here it comes.*

"'A woman of my age'? What is that supposed to mean?" Aunt Lucy asked.

Dr. Stein seemed oblivious to his slip. "I mean that as a woman ages, osteoporosis sets in, and bones tend to take much longer to heal."

Aunt Lucy slipped off the examination table. "Well I don't have any of that osteo stuff. I'm in great shape."

"I'm sure you are," Dr. Stein said.

The poor man had no clue.

"When should we schedule her follow-up?" Ivey kept track of Aunt Lucy's appointments in her notebook, and she pulled it out of her purse, ready to make a note.

"Never! I'm done here. Good day." Aunt Lucy gathered her Coach purse from the chair and stopped at the door. "Are you coming, Ivey?"

"I'll be right there." She had to make her apologies to Dr. Stein and find out about follow-up care. Even if her aunt wanted to ignore follow-up, Ivey knew how important it could be to a full recovery.

After speaking with the doctor, she asked the front office receptionist to send a reminder of the six-month checkup. What on earth would Aunt Lucy do without Ivey's help?

Next she had to go find Jeff and schedule their next meeting. They hadn't met since last week—a good thing since she'd needed a little bit of time after the french fry incident. But he was the other half of the subcommittee, and if she couldn't convince him to go along with her recommendation, she wouldn't get far.

Aunt Lucy had already walked out of the reception area into the hallway of the clinic attached to St. Vincent's Hospital and now giggled into her phone. She had to be speaking to a man.

Ivey marched toward her aunt, who still made googly eyes into her cellphone. Good grief. Aunt Lucy finally got the hint and wrapped up her phone call.

"That was Antonio. He misses me. Hoo boy, that man has the sexiest accent I've ever heard."

Ivey inwardly cringed at the mental picture of Lucy and Antonio and then felt guilty. After all, Aunt Lucy deserved to be loved.

"I have to go find Jeff—I mean, Dr. Garner, so I can schedule our next meeting. Will you be okay? It won't take long."

"Of course, dear. I'll call Antonio back. We've gotten pretty good at phone sex."

Ivey whipped her head around, grateful no one had been close enough to them in the hallway to hear her aunt. "Umm, okay. I'll meet you in the car?"

Ivey handed her the keys and hoped Lucy would take the hint. If she insisted on having phone sex, at least she could spare everyone within earshot.

Ivey had only begun to get the layout of the hospital and took the elevator down to the first floor where the emergency room was located.

As she approached the reception desk, a tall and slender redhead turned towards Ivey. Her name tag read *Donna—triage*. "How can I help you?"

Ivey introduced herself and explained that she was looking for Dr. Garner to schedule a meeting. "Is he around?"

"I just got on shift, so I'll need to check." She went through the double doors leading to the restricted area.

"Pssst."

Ivey turned, and an elderly gentleman smiled in her direction. "Did you say something?"

"I'm here to see him too. And I've been waiting a while. Name's Frank Sullivan," he said, sticking out a frail hand.

Ivey sat next to him, and then the Florence Nightingale in her took over. "Are you feeling all right? What's wrong?"

"It would be easier to tell you what's not

wrong." Frank tapped the side of his head. "Nothing wrong up here, that's for sure. Everything else, the warranty has worn out."

Endearing and cute. "I'm sure the doctors here can help you with whatever has, uh, worn out."

"Dr. Garner can. He has the magic touch. Every time I come here, I see him."

"Every time?" The statement implied he'd made multiple trips to the ER, and for his sake she hoped that wasn't the case.

He nodded. "He's always here, so it's not a problem."

"Yeah, that's what I heard."

"And what are you here to see him for, dear? You look healthy enough, but sometimes it's hard to tell." He cocked his head to the side.

"No, I feel fine. We kind of work together, and I need to talk to him."

"You're a nurse? Or a doctor?"

Ivey straightened a little taller in her seat. Frank hadn't automatically assumed she was a nurse. "I'm a nurse midwife."

"They certainly are turning out pretty nurses these days." No sooner had Frank given her his compliment than Jeff and

Donna both came through the double doors.

Jeff had a stethoscope around his neck and bags under his eyes. "Hey."

Ivey couldn't help a tiny twinge of sympathy for him. "I should have called you, but then I realized I don't have your phone number."

"Pssst, Doc, I would remedy that if I were you," Frank said from his seat.

"Yeah. Thanks, Frank. So what's up?" Jeff took a step toward Ivey, as though he'd give them a modicum of privacy.

"I want to schedule a time for us to meet with a local midwife in town. What's a good time for you?"

"I'm here most of the time."

"We'll need to go to her. Why don't I meet with her, and then I'll report back to you. Next Monday?"

"Doc, I 'm going to need some fluids today, I think," Frank interrupted from behind them.

"I've got to run. See you then." Jeff moved to give Frank a helping hand. "Donna, let's get Frank checked out. Talk later, okay Ivey?"

"Nice to meet you, Ivey," Frank said as he

shuffled away. "Be sure to leave your phone number with the doctor."

"Excuse me?" Ivey asked.

Frank stopped walking and turned toward her, then spoke loudly as though she might have a hearing problem. "I said leave your number with the doctor. Then maybe you two could go out some time."

"Frank," Jeff said in a warning tone.

"Well, Doc, you're here every time I come and you don't see a problem with that?"

Jeff didn't reply, his quicker pace being the only indication that he'd heard anything at all. They both walked through the double doors, leaving Ivey standing alone, wondering if Jeff wanted her number and why she should care.

"ITALY?" Ivey couldn't believe her ears. Aunt Lucy's cast had been off for four days, and she had already made plans to leave the country.

"I have to do something to celebrate the end of being cooped up for six weeks." Now that she was mobile again, Aunt Lucy used the energy to pack her bags. "And Antonio has rented us a villa in the Italian countryside."

"But we were going to start having fun. I was hoping you'd stay." Ivey fought to keep the desperation out of her voice, but the last thing she wanted was to live in this extravagant condo alone.

"It's time for me to move on. The leg slowed me down for too long. Anyway, you stay here and get that job you wanted. The women's center has been a long time coming, and I know you'd be great for the job." Aunt Lucy laid her minx coat gently in the suitcase. She tossed her last pair of Jimmy Choos into a suitcase dedicated only to shoes and then threw sweaters into another one.

"What if I forget about the job? I could spend every day with you. Would you stay then?" Okay that was desperation talking. Ivey wasn't going to give up the job and stay home and have one long slumber party.

"Oh honey, you don't have to do that. I'm still hoping you'll come to your senses and get back with your ex."

Oh, sigh. Would Aunt Lucy ever give up? "That's not going to happen."

"Are you sure?"

"Yes, and stop looking at me like that. I didn't come back here for him. I came home because you said you needed me."

"And I thank you for that. But you might want to ask yourself why you want to stay— you could get a job anywhere else. Maybe you did want to come back, and I gave you the perfect excuse."

No, she wasn't staying for him. In fact, he was the hardest part of staying here, since every time she looked at him she hurt a little bit. "We never did see that movie—the one with your favorite actor—umm, what's his name?" Ivey couldn't even remember now, as panic set in.

"I'll wait till it's on DVD." Aunt Lucy waved her hand. "You'll be fine. You can stay here. It's not far from the hospital, so it's convenient if you ever wind up getting that job. I've still got my money on you. You can do this."

The last suitcase packed, Aunt Lucy marched to the kitchen where she used the phone to call for a taxi.

"Do you really have to leave tonight?"

Ivey would have liked at least a day to get used to the idea.

"I've been cooped up in here for too long."

"You didn't even spend any time in the town itself. There are beautiful vineyards right here and people come from all over the world come to see them."

"You don't have to tell me. I lived most of my life in this little town. I talked Ben Cartwright into buying this condo so I could visit. They say you should never forget where you came from."

Aunt Lucy pulled out her compact and outlined her lips in fire-engine red. Presumably so that people would see her lips a mile away. Then she put her hands on both of Ivey's shoulders, the most affection she'd demonstrated in weeks. "I'm not like you and your mom, honey."

There it was again. Ivey hated it when Aunt Lucy brought her up or compared them. "I'm not like her either."

"Nonsense. You're so much like your mother. Oh, I miss her. She never wanted to leave the town where she met and fell in love with your father. Something about putting down roots. I could never figure her out either." Aunt Lucy shook her head and dug in her purse again.

But Beth Lancaster had made a habit of ruining people and relationships, and Ivey had gone behind her fixing what she could. Making excuses for mom, cleaning up the chaos. Protecting Beth from the nasty rumors. Unlike Mom, Ivey couldn't even drink a sip of alcohol without being inebriated, but that didn't seem to matter. When she looked in the mirror she still saw Beth Lancaster's dark hair and blue eyes gazing back.

The phone rang and Lucy picked it up. "Could you come up and help me with my bags?" She hung up and turned to Ivey. "Don't look so sad, dear. You have my cell phone number, and you can call me any time. And stay here as long as you like."

"But this place is too big for me."

"Then find someone to share it with. I know who that someone should be." Aunt Lucy squeezed her hand and then opened the door for the driver, waving him towards the bedroom.

"Stop. Why do you keep bringing him

up?" Couldn't Lucy see how much it hurt? Did she have to spell it out for her aunt?

"Ask yourself why I would want to come back to this god-forsaken town to recuperate when I could be anywhere in the world?"

"I thought it was because this is our home town. You grew up here, so did mom. So did I. We have good memories here."

"Honey, I wanted to bring you back the minute I heard your old beau was back in town and the hospital would be building a new women's center."

"You asked me to move in so you could play matchmaker?" And she'd imagined it was for her great nursing skills.

"Every two months someone in this town asks me for money. But when they came to me for a donation to the women's center, you better believe I gave them a sizeable one. Enough to call myself a benefactor. Doesn't that have a nice ring to it?"

"You—you did this? You're the one who wanted Jeff on the subcommittee?"

"Why not? You two needed a little push, is all. More like a big fat shove."

Ivey had left a fledging practice as a home-birth midwife. She'd left a decent apartment and friends so she could rearrange her life to take care of Aunt Lucy. Because she'd asked.

"I can't believe you did this! Undo it right now. Call and tell them you changed your mind." Ivey handed Lucy the phone.

"I will do no such thing. I don't mind telling you, you were one silly girl to let Jeff go. By now you'd be married with two or three little ones. Isn't that what you always wanted?"

And Jeff would have dropped out of medical school. He would have married her out of obligation, not love. Maybe they'd be happy, and maybe they'd be miserable.

"You can't do this to me."

"I can, and I did. You can thank me later." Aunt Lucy patted Ivey's back.

The driver stuck his head in the door. "All ready, ma'am."

"When will you be back?" Ivey managed to squeak out.

"I'm not sure. It could be months if all goes well. I'll be in touch. And I'm going to buy you a new car. No arguing. That old SUV is about to give out on you. Pick out what you want and I'll pay for it. Walk me outside?"

Ivey walked Lucy to the curb and watched the taxi cab become a smudge of yellow in the distance. She swallowed the lump in her throat and the memory that came back. Leaving seemed to be a pattern with Aunt Lucy.

In Los Angeles, Lucy had found a little cottage for Ivey to rent. Not that she had ever spent much time there with Ivey. After Lucy had made sure Ivey had enough money to stay for the remainder of her pregnancy, she'd murmured a few choice phrases about Gloria Steinem and the sacrifices women had made so that Ivey wouldn't have to hide a natural event and then taken off on her next adventure.

But Ivey wasn't hiding because she was ashamed. Not exactly.

She would take care of their baby, and within three years, once Jeff was done with medical school, she'd let him know. Then he could decide for himself if he wanted a relationship with their child. He'd probably be a little bit mad, Ivey figured, but in the end he'd see her sacrifice was noble. He'd see she'd done it for him. So that he could keep going forward without interruption. So that if they wound up together, it would be for the right reasons.

But it hadn't quite worked out. There was no point in rehashing the past now, bringing up old wounds and mistakes to examine them under the harsh bright light of today.

No point at all.

5

———————

By the evening after Aunt Lucy had gone, Brooke had already invited Ivey to a wine-tasting event. Brooke ran Serrano's, one of the more popular wineries in town, and recently she'd been so busy with their booth at the Grape and Wine Festival that she suggested Ivey join her at the winery so they could hang out. Ivey didn't drink, but Brooke Miller was her best friend and a person didn't grow up in Napa Valley without learning how to swish and spit. Wine tasting events and the annual festival were as much a part of the landscape of Starlight Hill as the river that ran through town.

Ivey, for her part, wondered why Brooke hadn't thought it important to let her know that Jeff was back in Starlight Hill. A little heads-up might have been nice. Not that Ivey would have let his being back in town keep her away from helping Aunt Lucy. That would have given him too much power.

However, his being in town was one matter and working with him on a subcommittee another. Her teeth hurt thinking about it. The last person she wanted to discuss pregnancy matters with. It didn't help that his eyes seemed to glaze over every time they talked about high risk versus low risk. Unless maybe he was as exhausted as he claimed.

His supposed exhaustion hadn't stopped him from checking her out. Yeah, she'd noticed. Several times she'd glanced up from her notes to find him staring. Never even bothered to hide it. And she was done walking in front of him. She could literally feel his eyes like lasers trained on her assets.

No, she wouldn't go there again, to a relationship that failed because Jeff didn't have time for one. And he still wouldn't, not with his resident's schedule. She'd bet a lifetime's supply of chocolate on that fact. Besides, he liked to plan everything and Ivey loved surprises. Adventures. Flying by the seat of her pants. Living life without regrets.

Brooke was behind the wine bar, wearing long dangly turquoise earrings, and a colorful bracelet in the shape of a snake hugged her bicep. Back in their high-school days, Brooke had worn her naturally blonde hair dyed black to match her mood, but now she was back to her blonde bombshell look.

"Hey, I'm here." Ivey sidled up to the bar. "And I'm not tasting."

"No kidding." Brooke of all people understood Ivey's aversion to alcohol. It wasn't that she judged others, but ever since Mom's accident, Ivey didn't drink on principle. Which made living in Starlight Hill ironic.

"Hey, Eric, I'm taking a break. And don't give me that look. I'm not even supposed to be pouring." Brooke waved an arm in a young man's direction.

"I thought you ran this place," Ivey said, following Brooke, who carried one glass of wine with her.

"I do. Which means I have to pour when we have an event and we're short staffed.

Like today. We're bringing in a new line of Cabernets that have a woodsy, nutty—you don't want to hear about this, and I want to hear about the job at the hospital. Did you get it?" She sat at a table and Ivey joined her.

"No. But here's the good news. I've been put on a subcommittee with a resident." Ivey explained the details.

"Well that sounds promising."

"Maybe. Except that Jeff is the resident."

Brooke froze. "Uh-oh."

"I'll say. I didn't even know he was back in town."

Brooke might have picked up on the accusatory tone in Ivey's voice. "Hey, sorry if I forgot to mention it. Life gets busy, ya know? Besides, I'm sick of you acting like you should be wearing a scarlet letter."

"I'm doing no such thing!"

"The hell you aren't. There's nothing to be ashamed of."

"I know that." It wasn't shame that had kept her away but more like a seismic change of plans.

"Think you can work with him on this subcommittee?"

"So far he's actually been kind of nice."

As long as she didn't count the midwives-as-clowns comment. "Even admitted that he broke up with me."

"The break." Brooke held up two fingers like air quotes.

"I'm going to make sure that we don't talk about anything too personal. He's already asked about Joe, only he calls him John to annoy me."

"It's almost like maybe he thinks imaginary Joe isn't real. Crazy." Brooke rolled her eyes.

Something pinged deep in Ivey's belly. "He's on to me? You think?"

Brooke shook her head. "I don't know if he would give it much thought."

"Don't look now, but your dislike of Jeff is starting to show."

"Oh yeah? Well I wasn't trying to hide it." Brooke had loyalty down to a science, but then again she'd resented the fact that Ivey and Jeff had been a couple all through high school when Brooke had remained single. Not through lack of options, which was a mystery Ivey still hadn't cracked.

"I'm afraid I'll break down and tell him everything. It'll come flowing out of me."

"After all this time? No, forget it. You need to stem that flow and keep your mouth shut tight." Brooke touched her lips on the word tight. "That's your business."

"Aunt Lucy doesn't think so. She still thinks he has a right to know."

"Lucy isn't exactly the authority of all things relationship-wise. Which husband is she on now? I lost track."

She had a point. Aunt Lucy had been through four husbands, three of them since winning the lottery. Husband number four was under house arrest in New York, awaiting trial. What did she know about long-term relationships? "But she has a point. Doesn't she?"

"Maybe she had a point five years ago. You should have told him. You were way too honorable for your own good. He should have stepped up."

"He would have," Ivey said and then wondered why she was defending her ex. They'd had plans, and they didn't include a baby. He didn't want to get married until he was done with medical school. Having a baby would have sent him over the edge. Besides, had everyone forgotten he'd broken up with her? He didn't want her then, and she sure didn't want him to come back to her out of duty.

"As usual you made it easy for him. Like you do with everyone. Think about it. You didn't tell Jeff because he'd drop out of school, you left your job in LA to take care of your aunt, and now I'd bet my Harley that someone else talked you into being on this subcommittee. Who is it this time?"

Brooke had kindly left out all the times she'd covered for Mom. *I'm sorry, Mrs. Monroe, my mom can't come to the phone right now. She's got the flu.*

"All right, so what? I try to help people. I'm a nurse. What do you want from me?"

"I want you to bandage a cut or deliver a baby but stop trying to fix everybody and everything. For once, will you do what you want?"

"It's not that easy. When I look at him—I don't know, he reminds me of what I lost. I can't help it."

Brooke squeezed Ivey's hand. "But what do you want?"

"I want to stay. And I want this job." Saying it out loud confirmed it, and for once maybe she'd stay, even if it was going to make things more difficult for her, for Jeff, and the rest of the blue-versus-pink-divided town. Too bad.

"Good for you. Then take it. Fight for it." Brooke pounded the table with her fist.

Ivey startled. "Right."

A hard-looking man with his jaw dialed to crush strode up next to Brooke and put a hand on her shoulder. "I need to talk to you. Now."

"I'll be right back," Brooke said as she rose, then called out to her coworker: "Eric, I'm taking a break."

"Hey, how long are you going to be gone? You have to get me some help," Eric shouted from behind the bar.

"Ivey, do you mind? All you have to do is pour and look pretty. You can do it."

Great. She knew almost nothing about wine. "You're kidding, right?"

"I'll be right back," Brooke said as she led Ivey behind the table. "Eric, here's your help. Be nice."

Eric, who didn't even look old enough to drink, glanced at her sideways. "So. Who are you?"

"Ivey. Can't that man wait to talk to Brooke?"

He lifted a shoulder. "I doubt it. He's the boss."

That explained it. Ivey had never seen Brooke rush to please a man like that. She was probably working on a promotion. "Help me out here. What should I do?"

"Push the Cabernet, and you'll be fine." Eric handed her an opened bottle.

For the next twenty minutes offering Cabernet seemed to be enough as Ivey poured and smiled.

She recognized some of the locals, but most of the people here would be tourists. The wine train made a regular stop here, and it was that time of the year.

"My heavens, Ivey, is that you?"

Ivey turned to see Wynonna Pusini, the high-school cafeteria lady. Most everyone in town referred to Mrs. Pusini as the town's spinster. Aunt Lucy said every town had one. It wasn't fair, but the label seemed to fit. Mrs. Pusini was a spitfire Greek-Italian woman who didn't put up with anyone's shit, and that was the main reason, she'd once explained to Ivey, that she had no husband.

Ivey stood up straighter and poured a glass of the red. "Hi, Mrs. Pusini."

She had to be retired by now, and she wasn't alone. There was a gentleman with her, balding with a slight paunch, his arm protectively around Mrs. Pusini's waist. Well, well, good for her.

"This is my husband, Al." She introduced Al, who took his arm off her for only a second to shake hands with Ivey. "I got married last year. Can you believe it?"

"Finally someone had the good sense to catch you."

"That would be me." Al nodded.

"What about you? Are you and Jeff back together? Please say you are. You wouldn't believe it, but I finally believe in happy endings." She held out her glass again.

Ivey poured her another taste. "No, we're definitely not back together. But we're friends."

"Bah! Friends? What kind of nonsense is that?"

Ivey blinked. Mrs. Pusini had had enough, and Ivey held back the bottle. That didn't make her too happy, if one were to go by the sour expression on her face.

"We don't all get our happy ending," Ivey said.

"Baloney. Look at her, Al. Isn't she pretty? What about your nephew?"

"What about him?" Al, bless his heart, asked.

"For Ivey. She needs someone. Isn't he about her age?"

"I think he's nineteen."

"Perfect!" Mrs. Pusini sang out.

Oh, for the love of Pete. "I'm twenty-five."

"Even better. You're a cougar." She cackled. Still smoked a pack a day, Ivey would guess.

She didn't like this new Mrs. Pusini. As Al pulled Mrs. Pusini along to the next tasting table, Ivey wondered if they still had a town spinster. Seemed like everyone was married or dating someone, if tonight was any indication. Except, of course, for her. She was the loneliest number.

Every town had a spinster. Could she be the town's spinster in training? Ivey wracked her brain for the last time she'd had a date. Back in LA, she'd given up hope on men. Seemed like every single one of them was either gay or an actor. But it was time to get back in the game. She couldn't take Mrs. Pusini's place. Someone else would have to do that.

Ivey bent over the bar and waved. "Mrs. Pusini, wait! I'll give you my number."

She waved back and smiled. Possibly she couldn't hear over all these talking, happy, disgusting couples. *Who are you kidding? You'd give anything to be that disgusting.*

When Ivey turned back to pouring, a gray-haired gentleman who had moved to the front of the bar startled her. He was also alone, Ivey noticed. Though maybe with good reason, as he had a stalker-slash-serial-killer vibe going on. It was in those dull, gray, empty eyes.

"Do you uh, want some of this?" Ivey offered.

He didn't hold out his wine glass but continued to stare. "What is it?"

Ivey swallowed, then smiled. Just pour and look pretty, right? "Wine. Red."

"That's fascinating, considering we're at a wine tasting event. Care to elaborate?"

"It's a—" Ivey turned the bottle in her hands, hoping she could decipher the label and it would tell her something. Anything.

But Mrs. Hughes's second grade class came back to her in Technicolor. She'd never been any good at reading out loud or on the spot. Dyslexia forced her to take her time.

"Miss, do you know anything about wine?" The man looked at her as though he could see right through her and the charade.

Where was Brooke when Ivey needed her? And did Brooke realize the irony in this situation? She'd told Ivey to stop helping people and then set her up. Damn, and Ivey had fallen for it. When would she learn to say no? Hell no. Well it would not be tonight, because something about this man made Ivey want to run and hide, not suddenly grow a spine.

She glanced over at Eric who was busy schmoozing with ladies who appeared to have had more than enough wine already. "Of course I do, sir. This wine is, um, dry?"

He took a sip, swished, and spit in a paper cup he carried. Gross. No one else was spitting tonight. They were swirling and swishing. But this guy had to spit.

"You call this dry? Has this had any chance to breathe?"

Did wine breathe? News to her.

Brooke rejoined Ivey then, easing her slender body behind the table and taking the bottle swiftly from Ivey's hands. "Mr. Dougherty, so good to see you. I have a case of the private label Merlot you wanted in the back. But this is our new Cabernet..."

Ivey relaxed and watched Brooke do her thing. After Mr. Dougherty had been satisfied, Ivey grabbed Brooke's arm and squeezed. Tight. "Where were you?"

But Brooke didn't have to say another word as Ivey took a good long look at her friend—face somewhat flushed, hair messed up like she'd gotten out of bed—*what the*?

"Did you just—have sex?"

Brooke pulled Ivey aside and shushed her. "Okay, you got me. A little quickie in the back. Thanks for covering for me."

Ivey felt the red color of indignity spread straight down to her unpainted toenails. "You drag me into doing your job so you can get a little action? I thought you were working."

"I'm sorry. My brain said no, but the rest of my body doesn't understand English when I'm around the man. Look, Ivey, I owe you an apology."

"You're damn right you do." She'd never leave a patient alone for a quickie. Although, okay, her patients did have a way of reminding her that a few hours of bliss often amounted to five times the amount of pain.

"Okay, here goes. When you and Jeff—let's just say now I understand why you ditched me."

"I didn't—" Ivey stammered, but her face flushed because they both knew it was a lie. She'd ditched Brooke on more than one occasion for Jeff.

"Back then I didn't know what I was missing. I was an eighteen-year-old virgin, and I didn't get why you and Jeff couldn't stay away from each other. Well believe me, now I do. You should have told me how—and then when the guy—how great it is when you both—Well, if I'd known how much fun you were having, I would have understood."

"Well, I—" She'd been in love, desperately and completely as only a sixteen-year-old could be.

Brooke laughed. "Okay, quit stammering. I didn't mean to embarrass you."

Eric called out again. "Brooke! If you're

not here in two minutes I'll be handing in my notice. And this time I'm not kidding."

"Sorry, got to go. He quits once a week, and even if he is a pain in the ass, he's good at what he does."

Ivey didn't know why, but it felt like everything and everyone around her had changed while she'd stood still. Sure the hills were in the same place. The ambling country road into town peppered with vineyards every hundred feet: the same. But Mr. Peterson was gone (good riddance), Mrs. Pusini was married, Jeff no longer had his nose stuck in a medical textbook, and Brooke was behaving like she'd discovered butter.

Meanwhile, Ivey still felt like the twenty-year old who'd left town with big hopes, only to come back empty handed. She still had the nagging, pressed-down feeling that she'd done something wrong, something unforgivable, even with the best of intentions.

She stood for a few more minutes watching Brooke pour and laugh with the customers. A few minutes ago Brooke had been with her boss somewhere in the back having sweaty sex while everyone else sampled wine, clueless.

That single thought served as a segue for sudden thoughts of Jeff and sex. Sex with Jeff. The type of thoughts she didn't want to have in her head right now.

Stupid wine. She didn't even have to drink it for it to mess with her head.

"Mommy says you don't have a girlfriend."

"Nope. What about you? Boyfriend?"

"No!"

"Ah. You're married, then."

"I'm not married, you silly."

"Don't tell me you're divorced."

"No!"

"Don't worry, someone will come along."

"Ew! I'm never getting married."

"That's what you say now. Your mother used to say that too, and now look at her."

"Becky! Jeff! Dinner's ready."

"C'mon, squirt. It's time to make conversation with the grown-ups and make believe we're interested." Jeff caught four-year-old Becky as she leapt off the jungle gym and into his waiting arms.

"I can fly!"

"Yeah, yeah." He plopped his niece on the lawn and watched her skip up to the back porch and through the sliding glass door.

Seemed like she'd grown three inches and several IQ points since he'd seen her last month. He didn't see his family often enough, so it was probably for the best that he didn't have one of his own. Who had time? Unless he wanted to blame the five-foot-nothing fireball that had come back into his life. They'd had a plan. Marriage, kids, the house, dogs. Maybe even a cat if he was feeling generous.

Medicine was now his life. He had to keep reminding himself that some choices required sacrifice. Even if he felt he'd already sacrificed enough.

Ali, as usual, was worried about him. She'd already seen Ivey back in town and probably understood the effect that would have on him. Ali said it was because they'd never had real "closure," which sounded like the psychobabble word du jour.

After dinner, he helped his sister clear the dishes while Bob the Saint put the kids to bed.

"I've wanted to talk to you about some-one," Ali said.

"You mean something." Jeff handed her a plate.

"No, someone. I met her at the park last week."

"No." Among all of her sisterly duties, Ali had become his dating service.

"She's a single mother of one adorable little boy. And a professional. She's a lawyer."

"Hate to repeat myself, but no."

"But why?"

"I don't do blind dates."

"But this woman is perfect for you."

Ivey was perfect for him, and look how well that had worked out. "Even worse."

"You're not making any sense. It's because of Ivey, isn't it?"

When it came to Ivey, it was true that nothing made sense. "I haven't let you fix me up for a year, and now you want to blame it on Ivey?"

"I thought I was wearing you down."

"You weren't."

"I hate that you're alone."

"I'm not alone. I have you guys. Scott, my roommate, even if he is gone half the time.

And the hospital. Don't know if you heard, but we're engaged. Very happy together too. I'll make sure to send you a save the date."

"This isn't funny. You're a great guy, a real catch. And even if you are my brother, the word is that you're hot. I know, gross."

"Disgusting. It's not like I haven't dated. I don't have time for a relationship, in case you hadn't noticed."

"I noticed. But sooner or later you'll have time. And then what? Are you going to settle down with someone because the timing is right? It doesn't work that way."

She wasn't saying anything he hadn't thought of at one time or another, when he had time to think about personal shit. Which was about ten minutes out of every twenty-four hours. Yeah he was alone, and he hadn't planned it that way. He'd wanted to marry Ivey right after medical school. He figured his wife would put up with the long resident hours and near poverty like no girlfriend ever would. He'd taken a lot for granted.

"What about one of those computer matchmaking services?"

Jeff couldn't help the tick that formed in his jaw or the way his hands tightened around the glass he held. "You mean like the one where Ivey found her perfect match?"

His sister had the decency to look shamed. "Obviously she didn't, or she wouldn't be back in town, single again. That's what worries me. You two are going to gravitate back toward each other like magnets."

While that had a nice ring to it, he had his doubts. "Don't worry about that. She hates me. The way she sees it, I broke up with her."

Ali froze and stopped rinsing the plate midair. "That's because she doesn't know, does she?"

"And she never will."

One month after their fight, he'd made it through exams and headed home to Ivey. To spend the entire weekend in her arms and never leave the bedroom. He'd been too abrupt with her in their last conversation. One week later he'd regretted it, but instead of calling, he'd waited and hatched a scheme to surprise her. Gone by his parent's house to pick up his grandmother's ring. His idea of a compromise. Ivey would understand how he felt about her. There was no else for him, but he needed more time to put his career in order. He would propose, and they'd have a long engagement. Ivey would get the surprise of her life.

Yeah. Surprise!

"It's for the best that she never knows, believe me. You two together were too intense. Young love. Bound to burn itself out in time."

If that were true, why did he still feel like he was waiting for that flame to die out?

6

"You can't be serious." Marissa Hartsell fixed Ivey with a look equal parts badass and college professor. Ivey was pretty sure that not a single one of Marissa's patients thought twice when she ordered them to push.

Even though her A Little Miracle office waiting room was filled with clouds of pink, blue, and white, Marissa didn't give off the same calming vibe. Ivey hadn't known what to expect, but it certainly wasn't this.

Marissa had managed to fit Ivey into her schedule two weeks after Ivey had phoned to ask for some time to talk about her midwifery practice. They were sitting on two chairs in the empty waiting room of the office converted from an old Victorian in the middle of town, and Marissa, from the looks of it, was not one bit thrilled by the idea of a staff of midwives at St. Vincent's Hospital's new women's center.

Ivey had explained the dilemma and her appointment to the subcommittee. She'd explained the doctors' objections to the idea. This was where Marissa should get on her soapbox and have a tirade about the unfairness of it all.

"Why on earth would you want to work in a hospital?" Marissa asked.

"Because I want women to have the choice of a completely natural labor without any medical interference."

"In a hospital?" Marissa nearly squeaked out the last word.

"I realize it doesn't sound like the best place to avoid medical intervention, but—"

"It doesn't sound like it, because it isn't. That why we're here, Ivey." She waved around her waiting room. "Women do have a choice. We're part of one of the oldest professions, working with the most natural event in nature. Well maybe the second most natural event, not coincidentally arising from the first."

"But women don't even think about midwives anymore. They're trained to go to doctors, and the option isn't really ever presented to them. Not often enough."

"We've done a good job of getting the word out around here. But some women are always going to feel safer within the confines of a hospital." Marissa lifted a shoulder. "I can't help those women."

"Don't you think it would be best if we could all work together? Doctors refer low-risk cases to midwives, and midwives refer high risk to doctors?"

Marissa leaned back in her seat. "Ah, so you're a dreamer. You didn't tell me that."

Ivey sighed. This wasn't going well. She was supposed to meet Jeff in an hour so she could report on the results of the meeting. Only so far it didn't look like she'd have anything good to say. "Wouldn't this give new opportunities to midwives?"

"New opportunities to be subservient to doctors. Let's face it, the hospital is their turf. They've earned it through hundreds of years of the establishment's rules. We've always worked in homes and places where women feel most comfortable. Let the doctors keep the hospitals. As long as they're in the same building, they'll never stop interfering."

Ivey hadn't expected to have this fight with a midwife. She hadn't been too surprised by the doctors' attitudes, but why couldn't Marissa see this as a new frontier?

"This is already being done in some hospitals in LA and other large cities."

"I've heard, and it's not working well, in my opinion. Too much medical intervention. Lots of fighting between midwives and doctors. Anyone who has ever been through labor knows that it's tough to get through it naturally. When the option is available for drugs and comfort, it's too tempting. Being at home removes that option."

Sounded like Marissa didn't have a whole lot of faith in women in labor.

"But what about complications?" Surely Marissa could see the need to be in a hospital for that.

"Ah, yes, for the five percent of low-risk women in labor who wind up having complications? Well that's when we transport to the hospital. But believe me when I tell you that I've never once had to take a patient to the hospital. That's because being at home reduces the risk of complications. Whenever pain relief is introduced, for instance, complications arise."

A half hour later, Ivey hadn't managed to make Marissa budge. When Marissa's next patient waddled in precisely at noon, Ivey felt as tired as the pregnant woman looked.

After introductions, Ivey prepared to leave, but Marissa quickly pulled her aside for one last parting shot.

"I wouldn't want to see you lose sight of what's important. A completely natural, non-medical experience for our patients. Anything less than that and we've robbed them of that joyful experience."

"Thanks for your time."

"Of course, dear. Anything for a friend of Babs. Why don't you think about coming to work for me here? I could always use an extra helping hand."

Ivey nodded. "I'll give it some thought."

She hopped in her SUV and it came alive with a pathetic effort, meaning she should have taken Aunt Lucy up on her offer to buy her a new car. The engine light had been flashing on and off for a while. That probably wasn't good. Next week she'd get it into the shop for a tune-up. Or a major overhaul.

For now, she needed to rethink everything. How was she ever going to convince the board to go along with hiring a staff of midwives? If Marissa's sentiment was the norm, she'd not only have a bunch of doctors angry for encroaching on their territory, but she'd also have midwives in a tizzy. And you didn't want to get a midwife in a tizzy.

Maybe she was going about this the wrong way.

Her SUV seemed to agree, as it made a screeching flappetty clackety sound. Ivey coasted off to the side of Merlot Highway. Perfect. Stranded on a sweltering August day. Wearing a white halter dress—obviously the perfect outfit for car trouble. She made the useless effort of pulling up her hood, always more of call for help than anything else. Like waving a flag of distress. Nothing under the hood made sense to her anyway.

With the hood up, she stared at the engine. Someone would stop and help. She should stand and look concerned. *Oh look, the thingamajig is broken. Dear me, I'll need a new whatchamacallit.*

Within a few minutes, she had her first stop. She didn't recognize the guy, so he might be a tourist. Then again, she didn't know everyone in town anymore. This guy looked like an auto guy, big and burly with a handlebar mustache. And probably no danger to her at all in the middle of the day.

"What's the trouble?" he asked.

"Ah, well. Not sure." Ivey looked down at the engine and shook her head. Like she'd tried to figure it out, but dang it, she was stumped this time.

She moved aside so he could look, but before he did he gave her a long look. "You're Ivey, aren't you?"

She tried to smile. "Do I know you?"

"Nope, but I know you." He rocked back on his heels. "I had a blue ribbon."

"Let me guess. You work at the hardware store."

He took a few steps back, shaking his head. "I work at the car shop. Bad luck for you that Dr. Jeff doesn't work on his own car. I'd help you, but I had a blue ribbon."

"Don't be ridiculous! Everyone took

down their ribbons ages ago. It doesn't count anymore. Are you going to leave me out here? Where's your sense of decency?"

"Where's yours? Date a Deusch.com over a doctor, lady? Anyway, it's the bro code. Nah, tell you what. I'll call someone else to help you. Someone who had a pink ribbon." He ambled over to his truck and got back in.

It was official. Everyone in this town was shit-faced crazy. Certifiable.

"He broke up with *me!*" Ivey shouted as the guy took off.

Ivey stomped her foot, took out her cell and dialed Brooke. She was working, something about the first crush, but maybe she'd answer. No such luck, as the phone switched over to voice mail. Was Ivey really supposed to wait here until someone who had a pink ribbon showed up? Would the insanity ever end?

No other cars passed by in the next few minutes. It was the middle of the day in the middle of the week, and she wasn't going to stand around until someone meandered home. She was only a few miles from the hospital, and if she didn't get there soon she'd be late for her meeting with Jeff. Late to tell him that the women's center might have to be fully staffed by doctors, because no midwives would come near it.

Lillian wouldn't be thrilled. She'd given her a chance, and Ivey couldn't blow it now.

Ivey rubbed her forehead. She felt a headache coming on, and the heat didn't help.

Whipping out her cell phone, she thought about calling Jeff, but that would take him away from the hospital. Sick people needed him more than she needed a ride.

She'd walk. It couldn't be more than a mile or two.

SOME PEOPLE CHANGED their mind every ten minutes. Ivey now wanted more of his fries. She had that familiar longing in her eyes, so he pushed the plate in her direction.

"Have as many as you want, Little Face." He couldn't remember the last time he'd called her that, but she didn't even blink. Smiled and licked her lips.

And since when did she wear lingerie to the diner? How had he failed to notice she wore the same red lace teddy he'd bought her from Victoria's Secret so long ago?

Damn, she drove him crazy. Always had.

He wanted to kiss her more than he wanted his next breath, and for the first time in years they seemed to be on the same wavelength. She joined him on his side of the booth, threading her fingers through his hair.

"Ivey," he groaned.

She put a finger on his lips. "Shhhh."

That's when he heard the buzzing sound. It got louder and louder as Ivey got smaller and smaller in his arms. "Wait. What's happening? Where are you going?"

When she disappeared, he woke up with a jolt.

Damn it. Sleeping on a cot in the doctor's lounge again. Alone. No Ivey anywhere in sight. Certainly not in his arms.

His cell phone was buzzing. "What?"

"Hey, Doc. It's me, Tim."

Tim? His mechanic? Jeff rubbed his eyes. "What's up?"

"Thought you should know. Your ex? She's stranded on the side of Merlot Highway. I didn't help her. Solidarity, bro."

What the hell? "Wait. Are you telling me you didn't help her because of the blue ribbon?"

"Yeah, and I feel bad. I was going to call someone, then I thought maybe you'd want to know."

"Tim, you should have picked her up."

"I can go back now. I'll do it. Whatever you say."

"Never mind. I'll go get her."

"By now someone else gave her a ride. Doc, she looked real pretty."

Jeff was almost positive she did, especially in this heat. Probably not dressed like a prairie woman today. The thought had him reaching inside his locker for his keys and grabbing a cold bottle of water from the fridge in the lounge.

"Anyway, thanks for calling me. You and I will talk about this later."

"Good luck. I really would like to get rid of the blue and pink ribbons. I have a lot of female customers that still won't talk to me."

"Yeah." Jeff thought they had gotten rid of them, but apparently Ivey's reappearance had dredged the whole thing back up.

"I'll be right back," he called out to the charge nurse.

He wasn't a mile from the hospital when he saw her in the distance, walking slowly until she saw him pull to the side of the road. Then she picked up her pace. It made him smile.

"Get in." He turned the car around, and hung his head out the window as he drove behind her on the shoulder.

"I'm almost there. Sorry I'm late for our meeting, but my SUV broke down." She finally stopped walking, turned to him, and damn if she didn't look like she could headline a wet t-shirt contest. Sweat dripped down her neck and had soaked through her halter dress, leaving nothing to the imagination, not that he needed any reminders.

"I got here as soon as I heard." He stopped the car, and walked around to open the passenger door. "I've got air conditioning."

She tentatively moved toward the car, for which he was grateful because he didn't really want to throw her over his shoulder and drag her into the car.

Her hand went to her neck, dabbing at

some of the sweat. "Thanks. It's getting a little hot out here."

Considering the trip computer in his car said the temperature was a balmy ninety-eight degrees, he'd have to agree. He felt stuck somewhere between anger with her for trying to walk all this way in the heat, and guilt that his car mechanic thought he'd been doing Jeff a favor.

Finally she climbed in the passenger seat and turned the dial up to Antarctica, pointing every vent in her direction.

"Drink." He handed her the bottled water. "Why didn't you call your aunt, anyway?"

"She's in Europe on vacation."

Ah, the constant holiday of the wealthy Aunt. "Speaking of your Aunt Lucy, why couldn't she use some of her bounty to get you a better car?"

"She offered. But I'm not going to be one of the people who are constantly taking her money."

Typical Ivey, always offering to help, never asking for any. "She is your *aunt*."

She guzzled, then turned to him with a pout. "Your mechanic wouldn't help me.

Something about the bro code. And the blue ribbon."

"Sorry. But he did call me, so his conscience must have been nagging at him." As well it should have. If it weren't for the fact that Tim was an excellent mechanic and Jeff was a doctor that shouldn't send people to the ER, he would have no compulsion with beating the shit out of Tim. Jeff could take him, too.

Ivey finished off the bottle, and as if she'd suddenly noticed that she was giving him a free show, she covered her breasts with her hands. "Oh. My. God."

He turned to keep from showing her his smile, and pulled out onto the highway.

"I guess you're enjoying this."

"Never."

"What did you tell everyone after we broke up? There must be some reason the entire town took sides. It must have been something you told them."

Of course she would blame him. "I didn't say anything at all. But I don't know, maybe I might have given off a certain vibe."

"What kind of vibe?" Her eyes narrowed.

That his heart had been ripped out by

the seams? That he was a damn fool? He hadn't said a word, but he was pretty sure his face had said everything for him. "The bummer vibe?"

"This isn't fair. There are two sides to this story."

"There usually are. But you're the one who left."

"And you left me first. That's the part everyone seems to be missing, because you kept your mouth shut like a typical man! So I leave town and some people assume I'm the one who broke up with you?"

Yeah, she was really fired up now. Too bad he loved it when she got all heated and outraged. It didn't happen often enough. "That's usually how it works. And you told everyone that would listen that you'd met someone over the internet and were going to be with him."

"So because I try to move on with my life, I get the blame?"

"Forget about it. This is what people in a small town do. Entertain themselves with the gossip mill. You knew that before you left."

"But why do they have to pick on us?"

She sighed and brought her hands down from her breasts. "It's kind of funny, in a bizarre way. Blue and pink ribbons."

"If it makes you feel any better, I think today's going to go a long way toward ending the problem."

"You do?"

"Think about it. Tim called me, and he knew I was coming to get you. He'll tell his wife, who'll tell her friends. And on and on."

"Right. They'll know that you and I aren't angry at each other, and maybe then they'll stop being mad too."

Jeff sensed an opening and he proceeded to drive the proverbial Mac truck through it. "The best thing you and I can do is show everyone in town that we're getting along. That we're friends again."

"Yeah. We better get the word out."

He nodded. "Having dinner with me might help too."

She whipped her head around so fast he worried about whiplash for a minute. "You and me? Not for real. That can't happen. We're not going there again."

"Going where?" Yep, he was going to do this. Watch her walk right into his trap.

"Sex. Getting back together. Do I have spell it out for you?"

"Wow," he said. "I'm flattered. But I was talking about dinner. You and your one-track mind."

Suddenly, absolute quiet from the passenger seat. But as his luck would have it, not for long. "I caught you staring at my boobs. Don't try to lie to me now."

"I'm a man, Ivey, and right now you're a wet-t-shirt-contest dream."

"Don't you dare stare at my boobs!"

He grinned. "Try and stop me."

She shifted her entire body away from him, facing the passenger side door. "I don't suppose you'd consider taking me home to change before we have our meeting."

Would he consider taking her home? This day was turning out better than he could have expected, but he was due back at the hospital. Eventually someone would page him.

He hesitated too long because Ivey changed her mind. "Never mind, actually. We shouldn't even bother with a meeting. Take me home."

This was a new turn of events. He'd

never known a time when Ivey would pass up a chance to talk. And she loved talking about pregnancy. For his part, it was all rather disconcerting. Early on he'd decided to steer clear of obstetrics when he'd done that rotation and witnessed a woman in labor scream like a hyena. He didn't do screaming women.

He'd always assumed that one day he'd be a father, and until that time he'd have preferred not to think about it. No such luck with this subcommittee assignment. He was elbow deep in all the gritty stuff that happened between two pleasant events.

"Why aren't we going to bother?"

"I met with the local midwife I told you about—Marissa. Let's just say it didn't go well."

"Elaborate." He drove well under the speed limit, and hoped she didn't notice.

Ivey turned to him. "It's not only the doctors that don't like the idea of midwives in a hospital setting. The midwife I talked to seems to think it's a crazy idea. The last place she wants her patients to be is in a hospital."

"Why?" Granted he hadn't specialized in obstetrics, but he understood and had studied how much could go wrong. It made sense to be in the hospital.

"Because this seems to be an 'us-versus-them' argument. I guess we're messing with thousands of years of tradition, and no one likes change. I thought I would get support from a midwife, because women who are too paranoid to give birth at home at least have another option."

"But again, why would women give birth at home when they could go to the hospital?" A stupid question, he was almost certain of it, but he dared to ask it anyway.

She blinked. "Haven't you been listening to anything I've told you?"

"Yeah. Listening." Mostly. Between, of course, the hard pulls of lust he felt every time she was in the room. But he could do more than one thing at a time, and he'd be willing to prove it.

"If you'd been listening, you would know that birth is a natural event, and it shouldn't be treated like a medical condition. The less intervention, the better. Unless absolutely necessary."

"You had me at absolutely necessary."

"Fair enough. It happens sometimes. Unexpectedly. We can't anticipate every problem. That's why I thought a good compromise would be the women's center."

"It makes sense. Why does the midwife object?"

"Because, as you said about your pal Dr. Stewart, she sees it as a slippery slope."

They sat in silence for a few minutes, then he spoke because before long he'd be pulling into the exclusive gated condo her aunt lived in. It was the only one in town. "So what are we going to do?"

She turned to him, the light in her eyes that made him a goner. "We? Does that mean I've already convinced you, Dr. Garner?"

He couldn't help but grin. "Congratulations. I think we should make our recommendation that the board hire a staff of midwives and let them decide."

She stared out the window. "I don't know."

He didn't either, because he was afraid he'd left something unfinished with Ivey. And it wasn't because he was lonely, but because he'd been an idiot.

He wasn't quite done with being an idiot. He pulled up to the condo gate, and Ivey recited the security code, which he punched in. "So—dinner Friday night? We have to make it look good. Make it clear to everyone in town that we're friends and they can stop taking sides."

"Maybe," she said, uncertainty wavering in her eyes. That one look hit him square in the gut, because he could see the worry etched in her eyes. She didn't trust herself with him. "You mean you're not working this Friday?"

"I meant next Friday."

Ivey looked gratifyingly disappointed. "That's right. I forgot you're not spontaneous."

"Hard to be, with a schedule like mine."

Now she looked guilty. "Of course. I didn't mean anything by it. But should we? This Friday, next Friday. Neither one is a good idea."

They'd have to agree to disagree on that. This was one of the best ideas he'd had in months. "I promise I'll behave."

"You better. Seven o'clock." She wrenched herself out of her seat and fixed him with a look. "And don't be late."

He wouldn't dream of it.

7

———————

Within a week Ivey's SUV had been repaired and driven back to her home by none other than Tim, who might have suffered a crisis of conscience. He left a pink ribbon taped to the windshield, in case she had any doubts as to his apology.

Maybe Jeff was right. It was a matter of winning the hearts and minds of every misguided person. Sooner or later they'd see that Jeff and Ivey weren't interested in anyone taking sides, and the pink and blue ribbons would be a funny story she could tell her grandchildren someday.

Of course, they wouldn't be Jeff's grandchildren. It was too late for them, even though that fact seemed to make her a little bit sadder every day.

Recently she'd had the occasional random thought that maybe it could work this time. Maybe this time he'd realize how much he loved her, and—great, she was doing it again. No. Just friends, Ivey. Friends, and nothing more.

Jeff had left the hospital to pick her up simply because he'd felt guilty, and not because he still had any feelings for her. He would certainly not be willing to rearrange his life for her in any way, to get married because he loved her, whether the timing was right or not.

He would go where his career took him, because that was of primary importance. It came first in his life, and she was a selfish brat for ever thinking she deserved more. Someday he'd find an understanding woman who would put up with late nights at the hospital. And it wouldn't be her. She had to be done with all that.

She'd turned over a new leaf, and it was all Ivey, all the time. Numero uno, baby.

Sounded horrible, but there it was. Brooke said it was a good idea anyway.

That's why she would do this dinner thing with Jeff tonight as he'd suggested. Because her own reputation was on the line, especially if she was going to stay here and make a life here.

When her doorbell rang on Friday evening, Ivey took one last glance in the mirror and then reminded herself it didn't matter a hill of beans what she looked like. Friends.

But when she opened the door, words failed her. Jeff was dressed in dark blue jeans and a white button-down, rolled up to his elbows. Casual but oh-so handsome.

"The security guy at the gate thinks your name is Iris."

"Oh," Ivey said as she snapped out of it. "Yeah, Ron does that."

"Ready?" Jeff asked, braced in her doorway.

She supposed she could let him in, but that wouldn't accomplish their purpose. They needed to be seen publically having fun, laughing, and being friendly. Definitely not kissing.

She grabbed her purse. "Let's go."

As Jeff's car passed the security gate on the way out, Ivey asked Jeff to roll down the window. She leaned across. "My name is Ivey. Ivey Lancaster. Not Iris. That's another flower. I'm Ivey with a V."

The man blinked. Jeff grinned, and as he rolled the window back up, he asked, "You're only now correcting him?"

"I didn't see much point to it. First I thought I'd be a short-timer around here. And after a while, it got awkward. I didn't want to embarrass him. He's been saying it wrong for a while."

"You've got to stop doing that. Worrying too much about other people's feelings."

"Exactly. That's what that was all about."

They rode the short drive to the middle of town in silence. Jeff pulled into Giancarlo's Bistro.

"This is where we're going?" It was one of the highest-rated Italian restaurants in Starlight Hill, known for serving the best wines in the valley. Giancarlo himself was almost a legend in Starlight Hill, having raised some of the best-looking girls in town and earned lonely attractive widower status about ten years ago when he lost his blessed wife. But Ivey hadn't really considered Giancarlo's to be the heart of the rumor mill. And also, it was mostly a place for lovers.

"There's a method to my madness. There's a chamber of commerce dinner here tonight. And Giancarlo's daughter Sophia is home from college. She likes to talk. A lot."

"You've given this a lot of thought. Perfect." Leave it to Jeff to find the most expedient way. He had more brains in his little finger than she had in her whole head.

There was a reason he'd been class valedictorian, and she—hadn't been, not even close.

Jeff led the way, opening doors and making her feel like they were on a real date. She should tell him to stop doing that, but it might be rude. Not to mention that she was rather enjoying it. It reminded her that she hadn't been on a real date with a real man since—she couldn't remember.

Giancarlo greeted them. "Dr. Jeff. Ivey. To what do I owe this pleasure?"

Ivey sized him up—blue or pink ribbon? Hard to tell. "It's not a date," she blurted out.

"Right," Jeff added. "Just dinner. I have reservations for two."

"Follow me," the gentle Italian said as he walked them to a table near the back.

"Could we have something near the front?" Ivey asked.

Giancarlo then led them to a table in the center of the room. "Would this satisfy?"

"Yes," Jeff said, holding the chair out for Ivey.

"Sorry, Giancarlo. But we need to be seen," Ivey said as she took the menu.

"Ah." Giancarlo leaned in, then whispered. "By whom?"

"By everyone, of course."

Giancarlo simply smiled and nodded, then walked away. He was the kind of man who never questioned anyone's quirks, and for that she was grateful.

"Blue or pink ribbon?" Ivey asked Jeff, pointing behind her menu towards Giancarlo.

"Neither," Jeff answered. "He seemed to stay out of it, somehow."

"Bless him. So how are we going to do this?"

"Let's look happy." Jeff smiled, and he did

look content. Didn't even look like he faked it.

Giancarlo brought them a bottle of white wine on the house, and after the ritual of sniffing and swirling had been accomplished, Ivey reminded Giancarlo that she didn't drink.

Still, when a couple she recognized walked past them, Ivey held up her glass in a mock toast with Jeff, who followed her lead. She smiled. Jeff smiled. The couple gave them an odd look and kept walking.

"Is this working?" Ivey asked uncertainly. For the first time since they'd walked in the restaurant, she took a nice long look at Jeff.

He looked relaxed. The furrow in his forehead eased, and he had on his lazy smile. She hadn't seen that one in a long time, and it so happened to be her favorite.

Maybe she'd done this. He was happy, free from obligations other than to his career. A doctor now the way he'd always dreamed and planned.

"Be patient," he said with that drop dead gorgeous grin.

Yeah well, she'd never been good with patience but always better at easing burdens, starting with Mama. Continuing with Jeff and their little bump in the road. Nothing had stopped his forward trajectory, thanks to her. Someday she'd tell him. But today would not be that day.

"Did you date anyone in LA after Joe?" Jeff asked.

Well. At least he got the fake name right for once. "Um, not really. I became a serial dater. No one special. And you?"

"Same. Although my sister keeps trying to fix me up. For the past year that I've been back, she hasn't really given it a rest."

Ivey squirmed. Yeah, she wouldn't be surprised. Ali had always been protective of her little brother, which meant that she probably owned a case full of blue ribbons.

"And I'm guessing that since I got back into town she's really stepped it up."

"Maybe." Jeff's finger trailed the edge of the butter knife. Ivey had never wanted to be a piece of silverware before, but at the moment she did. She had a sudden unbidden memory return of what those hands felt like on her skin.

"She seems to think you and I are like a pair of magnets." He met her eyes again, not for the first time tonight. But it was the first time that Ivey felt a tug deep in her gut.

She opened her mouth to speak, and a raucous noise came from the direction of the banquet room. A large group was filing out, which meant that the chamber meeting was likely ending, and they would be walking right by her and Jeff. Perfect.

Ophelia Lyndstrom, owner of the fabric store, was the first to see them. "Look at these two! Together again. It does an old woman's heart good. This is wonderful. No more ribbons. I've seen enough ribbon to last me a lifetime. Enough already."

"We haven't had the ribbons in years. What are you babbling about now?" Kevin Morrison, the cigar shop owner, came up behind her, and when Jeff and Ivey came into his line of sight he scowled. "Not this again."

"Our town can't go through this again. What are you kids trying to do to us?" This was from Henry Brandt, owner of the only market in town.

This wasn't going as well as she'd hoped. Jeff's expression said that he felt the same way. "We wanted everyone to know they can stop the madness. Ivey and I are friends. No hard feelings. No more blue and pink ribbons, and no more divided loyalties."

"That's right, Henry. It's none of our business if these two kids want to get back together, break up, get back together. They could do it a hundred times and it still wouldn't be any of our business," Ophelia said, waving her hands back and forth.

The rest of the Chamber members had gathered around their table to stare, making Ivey feel like a sideshow sensation.

She heard whispered words:

"her fault...,"

"blue ribbon...,"

"doctor...,"

"online dating...,"

"not a lick of sense... "

Enough. Ivey stood up. "All right, you all. Jeff and I are friends, and that ought to be enough for all of you. And by the way, in case anyone's interested, *he* broke up with *me!*"

All eyes then turned to Jeff, who sat rubbing his jaw, a slight grin on his face. "It's true."

"You never said that." Ophelia didn't look happy. Score one for Ivey.

"And you didn't ask. Plus, it was none of

your business." Score one for Jeff. Damn, a tie.

Some grumbling ensued, and within a few minutes the chamber members filed out of the restaurant, all one cohesive unit. Like a school of fish.

"Well I think we've got that settled." Now maybe she could enjoy her dinner.

"I do like it when you get all riled up." Jeff grinned, which did all manner of odd things to her stomach.

Their waitress sauntered over to them, and held her phone above her, bending down next to Ivey. "Selfie!"

Ivey was in the middle of the word *no* when the young woman snapped the photo.

"That was awesome. Okay if I put this on the Facebook page?"

"Ivey, this is Giancarlo's daughter Sophia. Remember I told you about her?" Jeff threw Ivey a pointed look.

"Oh right. Sure, put it on Facebook and Twitter, everywhere. Let's get another one, maybe one without my mouth open." Ivey brushed back her hair, smoothed down her dress, and sat up straighter.

"Dr. Garner, you get in there too." Sophia motioned to Jeff.

No need to do so, because he'd moved in closer without having to be asked. Ivey could already feel his warm skin next to hers, and he'd casually slipped an arm around her shoulder. Once that arm had been like a second skin, but now the sheer strength of it made Ivey feel like she had a barbell on her shoulder. She stiffened, aware that Giancarlo was looking on, smiling. Enjoying this little show they were putting on. Because that's all it was, a show.

Sophia snapped two or three photos, and when she was done, Jeff's hand slid down Ivey's shoulder to her waist, like it had any business being there. Maybe announcing their friendship to the town was a great idea, but it might be a whole lot better if he could stop looking at her like she was his dinner.

"Are you trying to cop a feel?" She shifted away from his touch.

He lifted a shoulder. "Trying to make it look real."

Right now this was all beginning to feel a little too much like a walk down memory lane. But she wasn't going to take that stroll again. Been there, done that.

Survived him.

But how nice to be out with a man who didn't want her to run lines with him or ask her whether she thought it was a wise investment to have his teeth capped.

Giancarlo brought their orders, and it felt good to be with someone who wouldn't question why she didn't drink. Who chose not to drink either, not because he had to, but maybe because he understood. He knew her history.

Jeff knew about Mama and her drinking. All about the accident that had claimed her life and thank God no one else's. He also knew that Ivey not only couldn't hold her liquor, but that after the accident she simply refused to drink on principle. And even though he didn't share her feelings, he respected them.

"It's actually nice to have dinner with someone who doesn't want to recite lines with me later."

Jeff quirked an eyebrow. "Actors?"

"All of my serial dating involved men who either were actors or on the way to becoming actors. I've had many different roles, I'll have you know. Unfortunately, mostly I've played criminals. Cop shows, you know, they're so popular. I've been a detective on the take, a hooker, and a junkie."

"So playing against type."

"My dates always had the best lines. It got old after a while. But I did have other, far more pertinent influence on the actors of today."

"Like?"

"To cap or not to cap teeth? To wax or not to wax the chest hair?"

Jeff winced.

He happened to have the best kind of man's chest in her opinion—a light sprinkling of hair, not too hairy and not too bare. Like Goldilocks's bed—just right. He'd never wax his chest. If he ever did, Ivey would know for certain that hell had frozen over.

He looked at her now, those brown eyes assessing her, making her feel emotions she didn't want to feel and have thoughts she didn't want to have.

Like what a great kisser he was, taking his time and savoring every second. Taking his time with—everything.

"So did any of these guys get work?"

Ivey cleared her throat. That's right, they'd been talking about her dates. What kind of a woman babbled on incessantly about who she'd dated in the past? A woman who didn't know how to behave on a date any more, that's who.

"I think so." Subject change, quick. No more talking about failed serial dating and men who were more fascinated with themselves than they were with her. What a fine way to advertise. Not that she was here on a date.

Friends, Ivey. Friends.

~

JEFF KEPT the smile in place, even if he didn't want to hear about the idiots Ivey had dated in LA. Not exactly the best conversation if they were on an official date, which they weren't. All the wishing in the world wouldn't make it true.

Even if he couldn't keep his eyes off Ivey, who was far more delicious than anything on his plate tonight. That said something, since Giancarlo cooked the best pasta carbonara in the valley, hands down.

Ivey. He had a distinct memory of what she felt like in his arms—soft, but pliable with heat. Not shy and retiring like she looked by her outward appearance, always dressed in sundresses and jeans like the girl next door. No, with him she'd been bold and self-assured. Wild and uncensored. Angel and Vixen.

They were good together, and if she hadn't left town the way she had, today everything in his life would be different. But by now he understood that he couldn't control all outcomes. Not in the hospital, and not in his personal life. Some things were left to chance.

"Ready?" He pulled out his wallet.

"We'll split it," Ivey said, obviously wanting to make it clear this was no date. Just two friends going Dutch.

"No. This was my idea. Remember?" He stayed her hand, so soft and small under his, and man, it felt so good. The first time he'd touched her since she'd come home, and it only reminded him that he wanted more. Much more.

Bad idea, because she was looking at his hand over hers like she'd come upon a bear in the woods. Alone and helpless, like freaking Bambi.

"Okay," she said slowly. "You win."

If only that were true, but they were talking about the check.

In a few minutes he'd be dropping Ivey back off at the place where Ron the security guard couldn't remember her name. Then he'd go home alone to his lonely bachelor pad. Now that Scott was off touring a baseball series with his brother Billy, he had a lot of quiet nights ahead of him.

It seemed a little odd to see the Channel 7 television van pulled up outside of the gated entrance, a newscaster speaking into a microphone.

"That's strange," Jeff said as he punched in the code he'd memorized.

Ivey held a hand to her mouth. "Oh no. I hope he hasn't finally killed her."

"Killed who?"

"Mr. Alfonso. They're our neighbors, and I've heard him yell once or twice that he's going to kill Mrs. Alfonso. Am I going to be called to the trial? I'm probably going to be the witness that says 'yes, Your Honor, I heard him say he would kill her.'"

Apparently Ivey's dates were not the only ones with a flair for drama. Maybe it had rubbed off on her with the actors and scripts. Because Mr. Alfonso was an over-excitable Italian who wouldn't hurt a fly, and Jeff would bet those threats were Mr. Alfonso's misguided idea of foreplay.

"Ivey, he's an usher at St. Catherine's. And this is Starlight Hill."

She turned to him. "But murders happen everywhere. I see it on TV every Friday night."

Jeff slowed down at the gate, where the guard wasn't his usual stoic self. "Miss Iris—"

"It's Ivey!" she shouted back to him. "What's going on? Why are all those reporters in the front? Who got hacked up or shot?"

That's it. Definitely too many crime shows. She ought to go to the nearest drug store and pick up a pack of cigarettes because they were the only killers he ever saw around Starlight Hill.

"No one got killed, Miss," the security

guard said, maybe finding it safe to not even attempt the name this time. "I'm sure it's all a big mistake. But they're waiting for you upstairs."

"For me?" Ivey drew a shaky hand to her throat, and for the first time since she'd been back, every protective cell in his body resurrected itself. This was Ivey. Ivey, who regardless of the way she behaved in the bedroom with him, was a freaking Girl Scout.

"Who's waiting for her?" he asked.

"The men from the FBI."

8

Jeff still didn't think Ivey had calmed down enough when they were inside the condominium, waiting for the elevator.

"Did you hear that? The FBI!" Maybe out of old habit, she leaned into him.

He snaked a supportive arm around her waist. "Calm down. It's a mistake. That's all it is."

"A mistake." She repeated, her eyes glazed over.

"Let's go up." Jeff more or less led Ivey into the elevator and up to the second floor.

There were indeed men in distinctive black suits with badges. No yellow caution tape. But a sign on the front door read: *Seized by Order of the United States Government.*

The audible gasp from Ivey meant she'd read the sign as well.

A gray-haired agent stepped up to them, showing his badge. "Are you Lucy Cartwright?"

"No, that's my Aunt. Is she okay? What's happened to her?" Ivey clutched Jeff's hand.

"Nothing, ma'am. As far as we know she's fine. This property has been seized for payment of debts owed to investors by a Ben Cartwright."

Jeff squeezed Ivey's hand. Everyone in town realized Lucy's last husband was under house arrest in New York City. The story Jeff had heard was that he'd been indicted in a Ponzi investment scheme. But if Lucy thought she'd walked away with this asset in their divorce, she'd obviously been mistaken.

"Didn't Lucy Cartwright obtain this property in the divorce?" Jeff asked the man.

"It's a common trick to pass over assets that way, but Cartwright's not getting away with it." The agent handed over paperwork to Jeff.

"If you've been staying here, we'll give

you time to get a few essentials. But you need to be out of here tonight."

"Tonight?" Ivey squeaked out.

"Go find a hotel room somewhere. Maybe there's someone you can stay with."

"You might have noticed it's a small town and there are no hotels." These guys were starting to piss Jeff off.

The agent shook his head like it wasn't any of his problem. "Mr. Cartwright should have thought of that before he robbed his investors of their savings."

Yeah, Jeff got it. He didn't like Mr. Cartwright either.

"Those people need to get their money back, of course," Ivey stammered out.

"Well, this will barely put a dent in it." The man said abruptly and went to confer with the other agents.

Jeff pulled Ivey to the side. He hated to see her this way. Confused, hurt, frightened. Again, someone in Ivey's life had hurt her. First her dad, who'd left Ivey and her mother when Ivey was ten. Her mother, dying in another small-town scandal when Ivey was eighteen.

Even he'd let her down.

"Where am I supposed to go now?" The look on her face, like she'd been gutted, slayed him. Maybe because he deserved it, he punished himself with the thought she might have had the same look when he'd told her that he needed a break. A break from her. That's how she would have heard it, when all he'd wanted was a tiny respite from the pressures of all the responsibilities.

"You can stay with me."

After the words were out of his mouth, he couldn't believe he'd said them out loud. But if nothing else, Ivey's wide eyes clued him in that he actually had. Not the way he'd once pictured living with Ivey. It would have been better if she'd chosen to be with him instead of being rescued, yet he couldn't see any other solution.

"With you?" Ivey asked, her right eyebrow twitching. She'd probably had one too many shocks tonight.

"I have an extra bedroom for a while." It made perfect sense, as long as he didn't think about it too much.

"I'm not going to be your roommate."

"Great, because I don't need one. Scott Turlock is my roommate, but he's out of town for a few weeks. It's temporary, until you get the job and find a place of your own."

"I could stay with Brooke." She worried a nail between her teeth and stared at the men in black.

"Seriously?"

"Don't look at me that way. I know you two don't like each other, but she's still my best friend in the world."

He liked Brooke fine, though he realized the feeling wasn't mutual. Daredevils like her practically kept him in business, but he happened to know she lived in a complex of Victorian homes converted into studio apartments, and it gave new meaning to tiny. He'd looked at one of the apartments when he'd first come back. "That place is the size of a postage stamp. You'll trip over each other in the hallway."

"You've been there? To her place?" Ivey's face reddened.

She couldn't seriously think he and Brooke—was she jealous? "No, but I am an ER doctor and Brooke is—well, Brooke."

"Stitches?"

Thank God, she believed him. "Stitches,

x-rays." He couldn't, and shouldn't, list all her injuries.

"She also has a boyfriend and I'd hate to be in their way. But wouldn't I be cramping your style, or love life?"

What love life? If she meant his sex life, that was one thing, but he hadn't had a love life for years. He was looking at the extent of his love life right now, and it was pitiful that he couldn't convince her to let him help.

"No, you won't be."

"It's not a good idea. I need wide open spaces when I'm around you," she added.

"It's not like you have a lot of choices."

"Wow. I've waited all my life to hear a guy tell me that."

"C'mon, Ivey. Let me help. Stay the night and we'll figure things out in the morning. You don't have much time to decide, because this offer is going to be rescinded in about ten seconds. And then what will you do?"

"I'll figure something out!" But she took another pointed look in the direction of the FBI. One thing you could say about those men was that they didn't look friendly.

"Yeah, and there is the park. Of course,

the bench isn't very comfortable, and Burt won't let you sleep on it. I tried."

"Look, I don't want to be any trouble."

"Ten, nine, eight, seven . . ." He began the countdown.

"Would you stop counting?"

"Five, four, three . . ."

"Fine! If it will get you to shut up, I'll stay with you. Temporarily."

WHAT WOULD the good people of Starlight Hill think of her now? What would Jeff think?

By way of marriage, she'd been related to a Ponzi scheme investor, which was bad enough, but now she'd been kicked out of her home. Practically in the middle of the night. Fine, the place would be sold and some of the investors paid off. That was only right and expected.

But now a bright light pointed to Lucy's ex-husband and the last thing Ivey needed was that kind of an association. She was still repairing her image as a love 'em and leave 'em witchy woman.

Ivey and Jeff packed up her bedroom, throwing clothes in plastic garbage bags.

One phone call to Aunt Lucy later, and Ivey had one more reason to be annoyed with her Aunt. She'd ignored all the legal notices forwarded to her because she had no interest in keeping the condo anyway. She ended the phone call by reminding Ivey that this was a chance to reconcile with Jeff, but if she insisted on being stubborn she'd send her more money. Ivey hung up on Lucy, and didn't bother telling her she was indeed on her way to living with Jeff, but not in the way she would have preferred. No, she'd be his roommate.

How could she live with this man and not be tempted every single day?

With enormous willpower, that's how.

Jeff surveyed the bags they'd hauled out of the condo. "We might be able to do this in one load."

She'd left everything behind in LA, and her roommate Sandy was only too happy to sell it off on eBay. She was still trying to raise money to get her teeth capped.

"All the furniture was my aunt's." She frowned in the direction of the men hauling out oil paintings, chairs, and a flat screen TV. "Except for this lamp."

Ivey touched the lamp she'd won at a midwife convention, her very first one in Atlanta. The pink, headless, and armless body of an ample woman, large breasts, swelled wide and engorged in the middle with the light portion of the lamp shining in the place of the womb. Quite possibly the ugliest thing she'd ever seen, but it held memories of her first professional achievement, and she wanted to use it in her own office someday when she set up her private practice. After first proving to the medical establishment that she wasn't a shaman.

"It's uh—interesting." The look on his face was a mixture of pure disgust and that ridiculously perfect grin of his.

"You don't have to be nice. It's hideous. But I won it, and it's supposed to be good luck."

"What is it, exactly?"

"A fertility lamp. And it should bring my future patients plenty of babies. Or at least a good laugh."

Jeff picked up the lamp, holding it at a

distance as though he feared it might actually work. "If you say so."

"Don't worry, it's going in my temporary bedroom." She took it from him, and placed it in the trunk of his car.

Ivey sunk further down on the passenger side as they passed the camera news crew on their way out. If she wasn't careful, she'd wind up being the news story. "I can't believe this is happening."

"It's not your fault," he said, pulling out of the gated community.

"But everyone will think it is."

His only answer was an unintelligible mutter under his breath, and they rode in silence for the next few minutes. He probably wasn't pleased.

Neither was she, since this hadn't been the way she'd pictured living with Jeff once before, when she'd casually asked him about married-student housing. He had made up some excuse about there being no room, and she got the message. *Not yet.*

She'd wondered if they'd ever get married. In the end he hadn't wanted to marry her, end of story. She'd been the high school sweetheart he couldn't shake. And now he probably didn't actually want her to stay in Scott's empty room, but he felt too guilty to turn her away.

If you weren't lucky or wealthy enough to own land in Starlight Hill, you were squeezed into one of about four small housing developments or one fancy gated community, built under protest according to Aunt Lucy. The city council kept a tight handle on progress, and not much had changed. As they drove, Ivey realized that she didn't know where Jeff lived. His parents had once owned a house in one of the newer tract neighborhoods in town. But now he turned down El Toro Street, and into what she and Brooke used to call Sweet U Lane. A smattering of pre-WWII cottage-style homes that were mostly rented by university students. The cool kids.

And even now, as Jeff pulled into the carport, Ivey noticed a group of girls hanging on the porch of the house right next door. Young, nubile girls wearing Daisy Duke cutoffs and guzzling beer. Basically Ivey's worst nightmare.

"Hey, Jeff," one of the girls called out. "Wanna beer?"

"No thanks," Jeff answered without a look in their direction when he unlocked the front door, carrying a bag of Ivey's clothes.

Ivey heard girlish giggles that trilled through the cool summer night air and followed them inside. "You can go with them if you want. I'll get settled."

He met her eyes. "I don't want to go with them."

Why didn't she believe him? Jeff was a single hot-looking guy and those girls were not shy about showing how available they were.

Together they carried in the rest of her boxes and bags, turning down help from the girls next door, who, to their credit, did offer. Probably so they could get a little closer to Jeff, and maybe sniff out what was going on.

Jeff set the lamp down outside one of two identical-looking bedroom doors. "This is Scott's bedroom. I should probably go inside and make sure he didn't leave anything embarrassing lying around."

"Please do." Ivey set down a bag of clothes outside the door.

After a few seconds, he came out. "This room is cleared."

There was an uncomfortable moment of silence between them as they stared at each other, and then Jeff ran a hand through his hair and cleared his throat. "You should get settled."

Ivey carried her bag in the room and shut the door. The room screamed military, which made sense since Scott was in the Army. The small twin bed was neatly made, with all the flat corners one would expect. Setting a bag of clothes down on the floor, Ivey took a seat on the bed. How odd to be here in a place that reminded Ivey so much of the dorm rooms where Jeff had lived. Every room and door so similar they were almost indistinguishable from each other.

Back then, she'd also been a temporary visitor too. She'd acclimated to spending weekends in surroundings that screamed testosterone: girly posters, beer, stinky socks. But she hadn't minded because it meant sharing a bed with Jeff, and getting all his attention for a while. He'd taught her how to please him, and she'd become well versed in the art of distracting him from anything else but her. It was that need for him that drove her life back then, but she was not the same innocent girl anymore.

She had goals and a direction. Unfortunately life had taken a left turn again while she'd been ready to turn right. But she'd roll, as she had so many times in the past. On the other hand, Jeff had a penchant to schedule everything down to the last detail, and all this couldn't be sitting well with him.

THIS COULD GET COMPLICATED. He wouldn't mind complicated if it meant seeing Ivey naked, but that was a pipe dream. This wasn't part of any plan he could have imagined. Ivey living with him, her bedroom inches away from his.

A few minutes later, he'd changed and pulled a beer from the fridge when Ivey emerged from the bedroom wearing a tank top and sweatpants that read *bootylicious*. In case he'd forgotten, which he hadn't.

They simply stared at each other for a minute, and then they both spoke at once.

"Are you going to bed?"

"I'm going to watch some TV." Ivey

headed towards the set and turned it on to the news.

Not a good idea. "Maybe not the news."

"There's nothing else on, and I might hear something about what happened tonight."

"Do you really want to?"

"Of course. I want to make sure they got the story straight. My aunt had nothing to do with this."

Curious, he waited to hear as well, and when they listened to a story about a boy who had figured out a way to recycle straws, Jeff had convinced himself that they'd skip the story altogether.

But no such luck.

"In other local news tonight, a Wall Street financial investor's home has been seized in an FBI sting."

"A sting?" Ivey cried out. "There was no sting."

They showed film of the newscaster at the scene, reporting on the few known details. Nothing Jeff and Ivey didn't already know. Then back to the talking heads, who seemed amused. Slow news day and all.

"I thought all they had in Starlight Hill were vineyards." The male anchor preened.

"Sounds like they've got crooks too. But even those are high-class." A light elbow to her co-anchor. A little chuckle.

Next, a large photo of Ben Cartwright and Lucy at their wedding. "Here's a photo of the couple in happier days. You know, Lucy Cartwright is a local who won the California lotto several years ago. It goes to show you, it's never enough." The male anchor shook his head sadly. This, obviously, was the news commentary portion of the show.

"For some people, it never is. But justice prevails, and tonight maybe a few unlucky investors are a little closer to getting back their life savings. Well, good night and sleep tight, folks." The female anchor winked.

Jeff turned toward Ivey, who hadn't said a word. She stared at the screen, mouth gaping. "Did you hear that? They lumped them together, showed their wedding picture for crying out loud, and made it sound like my aunt was involved."

He rubbed his forehead, feeling a headache coming on. "No they didn't. And no one will believe that."

"I'm going to call the station. This is irresponsible journalism. They might as well call it the evening rumors."

"You want to let it go. Let it die out. You'll only call more attention to the situation."

"I don't want people to think badly of Aunt Lucy. I know she's been married four times, and she probably has more fun than any fifty-eight year old woman should, but she's been good to me. And she's been good to the hospital too. That's something nobody knows. She's the women's center's main benefactor."

That got his attention. When he'd pressed, he'd been told that it was one of the benefactors who wanted him on the subcommittee. No explanation. Could that have been Lucy? "No kidding."

Ivey froze, then turned from him and snapped the TV off. "I shouldn't have said anything."

"She's the one that wanted me on the subcommittee, isn't she?" He would have a little fun with this tonight. And maybe someday personally thank Aunt Lucy, since he'd had more excitement lately than in the past year. "Maybe to get us back together."

"Why would you say that? My God, the ego on you! Are all doctors like this? Don't answer that. I happen to know they are."

She tried to get by him, but he grabbed her wrist. "Tell the truth. It will only hurt a little. It's like tearing off a band aid."

"I've said enough."

And maybe she had, because he had his answer. Aunt Lucy had played matchmaker, because somehow even she knew that they weren't done with each other. "Thank her for me."

"I will not."

"Then I'll thank her." He let his fingers trail up her arm and then back down again.

"I can't stop you." Her eyes didn't betray a single emotion, but he did feel her arm shiver.

Then his pager went off, because that thing had the timing of a metronome on crack. Reluctantly, he ended the standoff and went to find his pager on the counter where he'd unloaded it.

He recognized the ER's number, and called them back on his cell phone. "Dr. Garner. You paged?"

"It's Nancy. I thought I'd let you know

that Frank Sullivan came in and he was taken up to cardiology. Apparently there's something abnormal on the EKG. I know how fond you are of him, so I wanted to let you know."

"Thanks. I'll be right over." He gathered his wallet, his keys.

"Don't you dare. You've already logged too many hours, and the board will have our hide if they hear about it. I shouldn't have called you. Donna was right. And you know how I hate it when she's right. Stay where you are, Doctor, or I'll be forced to take drastic measures."

He let out a breath. With all the extra shifts he'd pulled, he needed the break. But this was Frank. How many EKGs had he ordered, all perfectly normal? What had he missed?

"Fine. I'll drop by to see him tomorrow." He hung up the phone.

"Is something wrong?" Ivey asked from the couch. She had a book in her hands now, something that looked like a romance novel.

"Nothing," he lied. Something was wrong with Frank, and he'd missed it. Maybe because he'd been too tired, working too hard.

Thinking too much about his own needs and whether the ER was where he wanted to land.

"You care about your patients, don't you?" This was said kindly, and took him by surprise.

"Does that surprise you?"

She smiled a little. "I wasn't sure how you'd do with patients. I've always known how smart you were, but not every doctor has the compassionate side of them fully engaged."

"I think they wind up being radiologists."

Ivey laughed. "We're not so different, you and me."

"Uh huh." Damn, he was tired. Not too tired to flirt with Ivey, but too tired to talk about what a great doctor he was. Or wasn't. The jury was still out. And he had an early call tomorrow morning. He took one last longing look at Ivey and made a snap decision. "Good night. I'm going to bed."

With any luck, he'd actually sleep.

9

Ivey blinked awake as the pale moonlight spilled from the overhead skylight. She jerked up, forgetting where she was for a moment. She'd fallen asleep on Jeff's couch. Her last memory was of fighting off sleep so she could read a few more pages. She'd almost finished the novel, and soon Melody and Bobby would be together again after all the trouble. They were meant to be.

She stretched and yawned. The digital clock on the kitchen microwave read four in the morning when she staggered towards her bedroom, eyes bleary and half-mast.

Once in her dark room, she fumbled for the bed and pushed back the covers. The bed seemed bigger than it had looked earlier. She snuggled into it, grateful for another few hours of sleep before morning.

"This is an interesting way of flirting," Jeff said from the other side of the bed.

What the hell?

"What are you doing in here?" Ivey rolled off the side of the bed and fell in a heap on the floor. "Oh, ow." This floor was so much harder than it looked.

"Are you all right?" He leaned over the side of the bed, shirtless. And who knew what else "less." In all their time together, she'd never known him to sleep in anything but a pair of boxers *if* he felt cold.

Ivey held up her hand. "No! I mean yes, I'm fine, and stay there! *Please* don't get out of bed."

But of course he hopped out of bed, flipped on the light and was next to her in seconds. "Did you hit your head? And why are you squeezing your eyes shut?"

I won't look, I won't look, I won't look. "I'm okay, you ninny."

"If you're okay, then open your eyes and look at me."

Please let him have some clothes on. She slowly opened one eye and then the other to find Jeff crouched next to her wearing a pair of dark boxer briefs. Okay, not so naked. But still. "I'm looking at you."

He gazed in her eyes intently—as if he'd lost his keys in there. "Where does it hurt?"

"Oh no, I'm not telling you that." He'd completely unnerved her with his penetrating eyes and his stupid sexy boxers.

"Don't be ridiculous."

"Let's put it this way: you're not touching where it hurts. Got it?" Her lower back had taken the worst of it, right next to her bottom.

"I'm getting you an ice pack." He was out the door before she could protest.

"Stop overreacting." She slowly rose from the cold hardwood floor and rubbed her butt. He had to stop behaving like a doctor and understand she could take care of herself. Nurse and all.

She made her way to the door only to find him blocking it, holding the ice pack in one hand. "But how did you manage to get the wrong room, Little Face?" He gave her a lazy grin as he leaned against the door frame. Her breath hitched when she heard his term of endearment. No one had ever called her Little Face before he did, or since.

"I was half asleep when I woke up on the couch. These two doors look identical. It was an easy mistake. And are you going to give me that ice pack?" She tried to snatch it out of his hands, but he was too quick for her and pulled it out of her reach.

"Maybe this is really where you want to be." He moved closer until he was only inches away, and she swore she could smell the minty flavor of his toothpaste.

She couldn't help but tremble a little bit, because he was so close, and dear Lord he was so gorgeous. The dimple on his chin. Words. Words would be good right now. "The—ice pack?"

"Yep," he said, but rather than put it in her outstretched hand, he reached behind her and held it right where it hurt. As if someone had drawn him a map of the area.

She jumped when his hand hovered near

her behind. Exactly where he had no right to be, MD or not.

"Cold?" he asked.

But also pretty hot, if I'm being honest. She put on her best smile through gritted teeth. "Take your hand off my ass."

"Sure." He handed her the ice pack. "I don't recall inviting you in here, but you might as well stay."

"I might, except that I'm not." She shoved past him and closed the door quickly, unwilling to hear one more word out of his sexy mouth.

She'd never make this mistake again, dark hallway or not. Maybe she'd mark her bedroom door with a glow-in-the-dark sticker to be on the safe side.

She didn't know what upset her most, the fact that he'd suggested she'd done this on purpose, or the frightening reality that for one moment she wanted to stay exactly where she was and find out if those abs were as rock hard as they looked.

No, the only way this arrangement was going to work, the only way her heart could handle this, was if they both kept their hands off each other. And if tonight was any indication, it would be a challenge.

The next morning Ivey blinked awake and pulled the covers over her head. Under the covers she'd stay until she could be certain he'd left. Wandering into his bedroom was not the way she'd planned her first night as his roommate.

One way or another, he'd get the message that they couldn't do a round two of Jeff and Ivey. A second breakup and there might not be enough pink and blue ribbons in the state. Anyway, one kiss and he'd see inside her. And he wouldn't like what he found.

When in the silence of the morning she heard a lone dog barking in the distance, Ivey tiptoed out of the bedroom and into the bathroom. Sharing a bathroom was another challenge she hadn't thought all the way through.

She would have to remind herself to check the toilet seat on a regular basis, because falling in during the night would hurt almost as much as falling onto the hardwood floor. She rubbed her lower back. Despite the ice pack, it still felt sore and bruised. Much like her pride.

The bathroom was organized better than she would have thought for two guys. And it was clean. The medicine cabinet had two empty rows—he'd made room for her. Well. This could work if he continued to be so accommodating.

His thin row contained only deodorant, a razor, toothbrush, toothpaste, mouthwash, and a small almost-full bottle of men's cologne. No hair gel for his glorious hair. No hair spray. So in other words, it still took no effort to look that good. Ivey frowned as she pulled out her toiletries from the bag she'd left in the bathroom yesterday—hair mousse and gel, hair spray, make-up remover, body spray, razors, special teeth-whitening toothpaste, deodorant, and make-up. Before long her rows were full and she squeezed a few more items onto his row, hoping he wouldn't notice since he obviously didn't need the room.

After her shower Ivey towel dried her hair. She wiped the steam from the mirror, viewing the face of a determined woman. A woman who had plans, a career, a direction. So what if she'd been alone for the past few years?

She would be all right, as long as she could stop thinking about him. Last night had been humiliating enough, but thank heaven dreams were private. In her dreams she'd stayed in that bed with him and enjoyed every part of his hard body. Even now, her naked breasts quivered at the memory.

Ivey pointed to her reflection in the mirror. "Stop it."

She dressed and looked through the bare kitchen cupboards. There were a few cans of soup and not a single vegetable in the crisper. A nearly empty gallon of milk, and some kind of science experiment that might have been cheese at one time. Ivey started a grocery list.

The man was definitely household challenged. Although he wasn't challenged in any other way. Highly intelligent, educated, respectful, kind, with bedroom eyes, and thick brown hair that she wanted to run her fingers through. That any woman in her right mind would want to run her fingers through. Broad shoulders, strong arms, and large hands that knew how to hold a woman. She did remember that. Abs to die for, she'd seen those last night. Ivey sighed, and then sucked in a breath when she took a closer look at her grocery list. She'd unconsciously written down every one of Jeff's attributes right along with the food items. She tore up the list and threw it in the trash.

What are you doing, Ivey? Fantasizing about her ex, that's what. She had to remember that he'd left her because she wanted too much from him. And he hadn't been willing to give it. Didn't want to marry her. Even if he didn't know she'd been pregnant, the fact was he'd never changed his mind. Never called and said he was sorry. Never told her he regretted their fight. Not a single phone call, text, or email. Maybe it was harder for her, because she'd carried a part of him, and that had made it impossible to ever forget him.

But sometimes Ivey wondered if she were silently punishing him for something he didn't know. She couldn't hold him responsible for the things he didn't realize had happened, but some small and unreasonable part of her wanted to believe that somehow he should have known.

Her cell phone rang. Ivey recognized

Marissa's caller ID and answered with a smile. "Have you reconsidered?"

"I'd like to talk to you about that. In person. Could we meet, maybe for breakfast?" Marissa sounded perky and excited. This had to be good news.

Ivey knew exactly the place. Sooner or later she'd have to face everyone after last night's broadcast. No better place better than Mama's to find out if she and Aunt Lucy were still welcome in town.

Mama's was bustling when Ivey eased into a booth at the diner, prepared for the worst. Em barely glanced at her, busy with the morning rush.

Ophelia Lyndstrom and Kevin Morrison were sitting in a booth on the other side of the restaurant, and as they were leaving, they veered in Ivey's direction.

She braced for impact.

"We want you to know none of us believes your Aunt Lucy had anything to do with that ugly matter," Kevin said as he took out his wallet.

"Not for a minute." Ophelia patted Ivey's hand.

"Thanks. Because she didn't. She's pretty upset about the whole thing." Over the phone from Italy, Aunt Lucy had some choice words for Ben Cartwright, the kind Ivey would rather not repeat in front of her elders.

"I imagine she is. The poor dear. You think you know someone."

They were being so nice it was a little strange. Where was the outrage? Aunt Lucy did know how to pick them, didn't she? Even Ivey would have to agree with that.

Kevin put his business card down on the table and slid it across to Ivey. "If you wouldn't mind, dear, give my card to your aunt. We need new advisors to the city planning commission, and I always value the opinions of reasonable people."

And Aunt Lucy sounded reasonable?

Ophelia nodded. "We should go. Have a good day, Ivey."

"You'll give her my card?" Kevin coughed.

"Sure." Ivey put it in her purse, wondering what city coffer or new project needed funding now. Everyone in town knew about Lucy's windfall, and had already hit her up countless of times for donations, investments or loans.

Em popped by to take Ivey's order. "What was that about?"

"I don't know, but I think someone needs money. At least they realize Aunt Lucy had nothing to do with her ex-husband's fraud."

"No one thinks your aunt had anything to do with that swindle. It's always the men who cheat. Always the men."

Well there was a story there, but Ivey didn't have time for it this morning. First order of business: get Marissa on board. She'd then start referring midwives to the hospital for work, and everyone would be happy. Possibly not everyone, but perhaps most people. Good enough.

"I was worried about you last night when I saw the broadcast. Where are you staying now?" Em asked as she poured Ivey some coffee.

"Um, well, I'm staying at Jeff's in the spare bedroom until I find another place."

Em didn't bat an eye. "Isn't he a sweetheart? I'm telling you, Dr. Garner would give the shirt off his back to any one of us."

Of course he would. He's rather fond of taking his shirt off.

She thought about those muscles, and what it might feel like to run her hand down his chest down to his crunch-worthy abs. To feel the strong beat of his heart under her fingers.

"So what are you doing today?" Em's voice jerked Ivey back to reality.

She was sitting alone in the diner, thinking about her ex's abs. Probably a bad sign. "I'm meeting a friend."

On cue, Marissa walked into the diner and waved to Ivey. But she wasn't alone. With her was a beautiful Amazon of an exotic-looking woman at about 36 weeks of gestation, Ivey would say, give or take.

Marissa made the introductions. The woman was Asia Foster, one of Marissa's patients.

"This is my first baby," Asia said. "And I want everything to be right. Perfect. I've timed it down to a science, and I should be having the baby sometime tomorrow. That's actually the anniversary of the first day we met. The labor will be smooth and progress swiftly, and then

I'll give birth right on my bed. My husband will hold my hand and recite a poem of his choosing right as our baby is born into the world."

Asia reminded Ivey of Jeff on steroids. The woman liked to plan too, and unfortunately would soon find out that babies did the planning. And didn't tell you about it ahead of time. Not to mention the fact that according to everything Babs said, they continued to do that for the next few years of their lives.

Ivey and Marissa exchanged a meaningful look, fine-tuned by midwives all around the world. *How precious. First time mothers. Gotta love them.*

"What makes you think you're going to give birth tomorrow?" Ivey asked.

"Months of visualizing techniques. Works every time."

"So the problem is," Marissa said, with a look that implied this would be no problem at all, "I'm going out of town tomorrow to visit my sister in Oregon. I hate the Grape & Wine Festival. All those people worshipping a vine. It's ridiculous. So Asia is a little bit worried."

"A lot worried. You're my midwife. Who knew you'd be taking off when I give birth?"

"This is Asia's first baby, and I've tried to explain babies have their own time table, and being that she's barely now at thirty-eight weeks gestation, it's highly unlikely the baby will come tomorrow. And I'll be back Monday morning. But my idea, Ivey, is that you would cover for me while I'm gone. To ease Asia's mind. Again, I doubt that the baby will come—"

"Oh he's coming," Asia said with a slight whistle.

Because Ivey had never met a mother who could determine her baby's day of birth, she was 99.9% certain that covering for Marissa would mean maybe a phone call from Asia asking why nothing was happening and not much beyond that.

"I'd love to. Don't worry, Asia, if your baby—"

"*When*, you mean."

"Sure. When your baby comes, I'll be there." Ivey leaned over to pat the woman's hand, an empathy trick she'd learned from Babs.

Asia's eyes narrowed. "But you don't look old enough to be a midwife."

"I've already gone over Ivey's qualifications. She studied under a colleague, Babs Holiday. I trust her completely."

Fortunately, it didn't look like either one of the women had seen the news last night or made the connection between Aunt Lucy and Ivey, or maybe they'd have other thoughts.

To put Asia at ease, Ivey went over her experience and qualifications again. All the skills she'd put on the back burner for the past few weeks that she'd been back in town —first taking care of Aunt Lucy and now fighting for a job in a hospital. Fighting to be acknowledged. But it occurred to her that she missed bringing babies into the world. Even though Asia's baby would not be arriving on her watch, she had to get back to the business of birth sooner rather than later. This was probably Marissa's gentle way of reminding Ivey where her priorities should be, and she did have a point.

Asia finally left with Marissa, reassured that her baby wouldn't be brought into the world by an incompetent. Now Ivey could get to the grocery store and take care of someone else's incompetence.

"You're kidding! But it's for the kids! How can you do this to me on such short notice?" Em shouted into the phone. The diner did take-out orders, and Ivey wondered what kind of an order would elicit that kind of re-action. "That's a fine how-de-do. Yeah, yeah. Goodbye."

Ivey picked up her ticket and swung by the register to pay. "What was that about?"

"My niece informs me she can't come down and help me with our booth at the fes-tival like she does every year. Leaves me hanging the day before. How do you like that?"

Ivey would be dropping by the festival, because that's what people in Starlight Hill did. She'd make an appearance, say hello to everyone so they realized she wasn't judging them for loving the vine, and then leave. Maybe she'd rent a movie afterwards or download another book for her Kindle. Great, she was starting to sound like the town spinster.

Em was eyeing Ivey in a way she never

had before, sizing her up. "Are you about a size six?"

Ivey cleared her throat. More like a size seven. Her "girls" kept her from the smaller sizes, since they had their own zip code. "Er, about that. Why?"

"I have to ask you for a huge favor. It's for a good cause, and I know you'll be perfect for it."

With that, Ivey braced herself once again.

10

"She has got to be kidding," Ivey muttered the following day as she inspected the costume she'd promised to wear to the festival.

She'd agreed to help out at Em and Si's booth—some kind of Medieval theme—and that meant wearing a costume. Because she wanted to show how much she appreciated the town's support, and also because it was a bit difficult to say no to Em, Ivey agreed to pitch in. It would mean that she'd meet some people at least, and wasn't that what a woman intent on not being the town's spinster should do every once in a while? Sounded like a good idea at the time.

Big mistake. Unless the intent was to look like a Swiss Miss in a size-too-small top. *That's the last time you lie about being a size six.*

The tight, off-the-shoulder white top and black lace-up waist cincher pressed down on her like a vice, her body ready to bust out at any given moment. The red skirt was short, which would at least be a relief during the scorcher predicted today. The outfit was completed with a red scarf and fishnet stockings which were definitely not going on her legs. A girl had to have some pride.

"You're helping a friend," she reminded herself in the mirror. She tiptoed out of her bedroom. If she timed things right, she could get out of the house before Jeff got a glimpse of her.

No such luck, as she passed Jeff in the kitchen, drinking some of the milk she'd purchased. That same milk nearly came spewing out of his mouth. "Holy Swiss Miss. Wow."

"Stop staring. This can't be a size six, or maybe it shrunk. This doesn't fit," she said as she pulled up on the top, glossing over the fact that she hadn't worn a size six since high school.

"Oh, it fits." He grinned.

Since he wore low slung jeans and a gray baseball team jersey, she got the message that he wasn't on his way to work. "You're not going to the festival, are you?"

"I'm stopping by the hospital first, but I'll be there later." He folded his arms and leaned against the kitchen counter. "The whole town goes to the festival. You ought to remember."

"Right. See you there." She didn't like that gleam in his eyes. It told her maybe there was something else. Something she didn't know. But damned if she was going to indulge him by asking.

Ninety degrees at nine in the morning was never a good omen, but there it loomed displayed on the trip computer of her SUV. *August in California.* Anyone in their right mind would be in their air-conditioned home, or seeking AC elsewhere. The rest of them would be at the festival. Drinking.

Burt the police chief would be out tonight, making sure everyone took advantage of the free rides he provided in the back of his cruiser.

Wine tasting booths from the local vineyards were set up all around the center of town, prepared to sell out of chilled white wine and even some of the red stuff—Cabernet or whatever. There were booths with oil paintings from local artists and handmade leather boots and belts from the Williamson family. Balloons and cotton candy for the kids and lots of beer on tap for the few people who didn't do wine. In the distance, a crew worked to set the stage for the bands that would play tonight. Brooke would be in the crowd somewhere. Ivey hadn't seen much of her lately.

When she reached the diner's booth, Ivey waved her arm from her top to the bottom of the short skirt. Si wouldn't even look at her. "Is this some kind of a joke?"

"You look great." Em was dressed in a matronly Renaissance gown, more of what Ivey had in mind. Em caught her eyeing her gown. "You don't want to be in this. It's too hot."

But then Ivey saw another sign—a sign which caused her to hitch her breath and break out in a sweat that had little to do with the weather. *No.* Ivey picked up the small sign, waving it at Em. "What—exactly—is *this*?" The sign read *Kisses from Swiss Miss - $1.00. All proceeds go to St. Vincent's Home for Unwed Mothers.*

"Isn't it wonderful? My niece does this every year. It's for a good cause, and with you being a midwife, I knew you'd want to help out," Em said with a straight face.

"This is why you thought I'd be perfect?"

"Consider it a compliment, dear. We always get the prettiest and best endowed girl we can find. Like I said, my niece, Miss California, couldn't come out this year."

Best endowed? "I don't like this at all." She was no beauty queen and her endowments would get far too much sun in this getup. "Can't I help you serve the food?"

"It's a kiss on the cheek, for goodness' sake. I'm not running a brothel," Em said with a laugh.

If that were true, why did Ivey feel dressed to work in one?

Before long, a line formed at their booth, and Ivey reluctantly settled in behind the counter.

Sometimes an entire family came up to order, donating a dollar without collecting a kiss, but every now and again there was the random teenage boy standing in line. Ivey became nervous and self-conscious about her PG-13 rated clothing, and threw occasional pointed looks in Em's direction. The boys were mostly perfect gentlemen as they turned their cheek for a kiss, and only later did she see them point in her direction, making her feel sixteen all over again.

Adding to the feeling of being sixteen was noting Jeff in the line near the end of the day. Before long he'd somehow made his way to the front, skipping ahead of several customers with ease. Most of them seem to know and like him, calling him "Doc" and letting him cut in line.

Jeff ordered Pirate's Grog and a smoked-beef-brisket sandwich and paid Em. Then he handed Ivey a ten-dollar bill.

"That's very generous of you, but you can't have ten kisses," she said, taking the bill from his hand. "I think it's against the rules."

"How about a ten dollar kiss then?" He grinned.

Some of the men behind him whooped and laughed.

"You can't have that either."

"Be reasonable," he said, pointing to his cheek and leaning in closer.

People were beginning to stare at their exchange, including Em and Si. The bigger deal Ivey made out of a simple kiss, the more attention she would call to it. She'd have to play along even if the thought of kissing him made her knees feel like Jell-O on a hot day.

"Fine," she said, leaning forward. "A ten dollar kiss."

Her heart did a flip as she and Jeff drew closer than they'd been in years. She aimed for his cheek, but did not expect him to take her face in his hands as though he would be the one doing the kissing. Too late she saw him headed straight for her lips, but as their noses touched Ivey whispered, "Don't."

Her tone must have been pleading enough, and his eyes gazed into hers with what seemed to be a quiet agreement and his lips turned toward her cheek. Ivey closed her eyes as his prickly chin touch her face, causing more shivers to run down her spine. He kissed her lightly on the cheek as one hand held the back of her head, his fingers threading through her hair. His lips felt hot like a brand, and she prayed the soft moan hadn't really come out of her throat. Time seemed to suspend and Ivey couldn't stop herself from resting her hand on his shoulder. His very smell was too familiar, the memory of him far too intoxicating, until she forced herself to pull away.

"There! A ten-dollar kiss." She turned to find a small crowd staring, including Si, his jaw slack.

Em slammed the Pirate's Grog in front of Jeff, her lips a thin straight line. "No more ten-dollar kisses, Doc. Any more of that and the two of you need to get a room."

As dusk settled over the park and the band began to play, Ivey was issued a reprieve from her duties. After a moment to change into her well-worn jeans and tank top, Ivey headed out to the lawn with her blanket to find a good spot.

Brooke was at the Serrano booth, serving up drinks with the same man who had spirited her away. The boss who had the hots for her.

"About time you dropped by," Brooke called out.

"I've been busy helping at Em's booth."

"So I heard. And saw the outfit." Brooke grinned. "How'd you get roped into that?"

"Don't start with me. I didn't know about the costume until it was too late."

"And knowing you, you weren't going to bail on her at the last minute."

"Well, no."

"I'll be working till we're done here, but we'll catch up later," Brooke said.

But Brooke seemed too caught up with the boss to want to spend any time with Ivey. And if it were really love, Ivey couldn't blame her, except that from where she stood it looked more like lust than anything else. Brooke might well be the only woman who could keep her heart from being involved, but even so Ivey had her doubts.

She found an empty spot to spread her blanket out and wait for the band to play, as all around her couples sat wrapped in each other's arms. Maybe if she sat here for a while, she wouldn't be alone for long. But alone or not, she'd be okay. *Keep telling yourself that.*

ALL RIGHT, so Jeff may have pushed a bit too far with the ten-dollar kiss. Only Ivey had the ability to turn him into a testosterone-driven horny adolescent. It hadn't even been Ivey's plea that stopped him from kissing her on the lips, but the sudden realization that he was about to set a precedent, and he sure as hell didn't want anyone else paying for a ten dollar kiss.

He stayed in the shadows, searching for Ivey. He spotted her sitting on a blanket, wearing jeans the way only she could wear them and a pink tank top that displayed the great rack that still headlined his fantasies. He wasn't surprised to see she'd become a quick-change artist, but a little bit unnerved by how she still made his heart pound.

Relationships weren't like hitting the pause button and resuming again. Even though it felt that way at times—like no time at all passed. Like the whole separation had been a mistake.

Was Ivey right about the fact that they couldn't do this again? Did Ali make sense when she thought he ought to stay away? No matter what his head said, his heart seemed to have other ideas. He'd never let it lead before, but maybe it was time.

Ivey's long dark hair caught a glint of the moonlight, but there was a slight problem with the picture. Mr. Williamson's boy Jimmy, who had to be all of eighteen-years-old, sat with her on the blanket. Jimmy had hopes of touching heaven too, and Jeff almost felt sorry for him as he prepared to dash those dreams.

"Hey, Jimmy. So, your mom is calling you. Something about watching your sister while they pack up," Jeff lied as he emerged from the shadows. Something told him that Mrs. Williamson wasn't going to object to some help with her youngest, and Jimmy would only look like a good son thanks to him. No harm, no foul.

Jimmy's face fell as he rose from the blanket. *Ah yes, so close and yet so far. Sorry, buddy.*

"See you later, Ivey. Don't forget my band is playing tomorrow night."

"Okay, Jimmy, I'll be sure to clap the loudest."

Jimmy smiled as though he'd won the lottery.

Jeff sat down beside Ivey. "How dare you? He's a child."

"What? I didn't do any—" Ivey protested. "Oh. You're teasing me."

"I'm sorry, but you make it easy sometimes."

"That was a mean thing to do today. Do you know how hard it was for me to stand there looking like the town wench while teenage boys ogled me?" Ivey slapped his shoulder.

"I know how hard it was for me," he said.

"You and your ten-dollar kiss." Her words scolded, but her eyes were smiling.

"You can't blame a guy for trying."

Ivey turned her head toward the music again, as the band broke out into Lionel Ritchie's song *Truly*. Couples began to slow dance to the song. Jeff sucked in a breath through clenched teeth, and his gut pinched with envy. He was so tired of being alone, so weary of the temporary nature of every relationship he'd had since Ivey.

"So what made you go online to find the perfect love match?"

She turned to him, her posture suddenly

defensive. "Why would you ask me that now? Don't you believe me?"

"Believe what?"

"That I found someone online."

"Why wouldn't I believe you? My question is why. Isn't that supposed to be the move of the desperate?"

Ivey fingered the threads of fringe on her blanket. "Leave it to you to make fun of people who need a little help in the love department. You probably never had any trouble getting a date."

"I didn't think you would either."

"Shows you how much you know."

"All right, fine. I'm not judging you or anyone else who uses those services. It takes all the fun out of it. Doesn't it?" Sure, he believed in planning, but even he realized you couldn't plan who you fell in love with.

He'd known that the first time he met Ivey, who'd nearly chopped off her finger in a high school Home Ec cooking class. He'd been the one tasked to take her to the office for first aid, which he'd administered himself when the health clerk had been otherwise occupied.

"Don't you know how to hold a knife?"

he'd asked, his bedside manner at the time sadly lacking.

"I guess not," she'd answered as she smiled at him through watery eyes. "Thanks for helping me."

He'd looked at her. Really seen her for the first time. He didn't see Beth Lancaster's daughter, the dyslexic girl who'd been placed in an at-risk group early on. He only saw Ivey, and something in his heart had pinched and constricted.

He'd never been the same again.

"As someone who plans, you should try online dating. You can pick the qualities you want in a mate."

He supposed that was a dig, but a person didn't get an MD after their name without some preparation.

"I'll pass. But if I'd been able to pick from a list of qualities, I might have picked someone who could cook." Unless it came out of a can or a box, Ivey would have starved to death.

"Funny."

"Is that what you did? Looked at a list of qualities you wanted and checked them off one by one?"

She sighed. "I don't want to talk about this anymore."

Well if they weren't going to talk, he had some other ideas of how to fill the time. He stood, taking his chances, and held out his hand. "Dance?"

Ivey rose to meet him. "You want to dance? But you don't know how. Have you learned?"

"All right, you got me. Not really, but I want to hold you tight."

"At least you're honest." She didn't resist when he took her in his arms right there on the blanket and pressed her against him. He held his hands near the small of her back, and her arms rose to his neck, as she gazed right into his eyes. He swallowed hard.

He couldn't still love her. Could he? Love didn't stay in a suspended state of animation for years and then suddenly surge to the front. This was lust, pure and simple. He had it bad for Ivey. Always had.

"Hey, do you remember when we used to listen to concerts here?" Ivey smiled up at him.

He did. And if he didn't stop thinking about that, he would soon be too hard to continue this slow dance of torture. "Yeah," he managed to say. *He'd forgotten his brain stopped working when she was this close.*

He ran a hand through her hair, the silkiness making his fingers feel like sandpaper. Ivey gazed up at him, but he couldn't figure out if what he saw in her eyes was desire or plain confusion. Still, he took his opening and bent down and covered her mouth with his. He tried not to groan as her mouth opened in welcome and he deepened the kiss. She tasted like vanilla and memories, the best ones—long summer nights by the river when the choice between her and *Gray's Anatomy* had been a no-brainer. Funny how the pain she had caused him faded into the background now.

He could feel her hands clinging to him like she used to when she'd been filled with need, but her fingers shook as they wrapped around his arms. "You're trembling," he said, stroking the curve of her face.

"I'm sorry," she whispered. "You do that to me."

"Yeah? Totally flattered." It took him a minute to realize the song had ended and the rest of the crowd danced to a different one he didn't even recognize.

Still they stood holding each other like maybe they were trying to make up for lost time. He leaned his forehead against Ivey's and heard her sigh. A warm summer night, the hint of honeysuckle in the air, Ivey in his arms at last. It was too perfect.

Which is why it shouldn't have surprised him when Ali walked up and almost wedged herself between them. "Hi, Ivey. Welcome back."

"Ali," Ivey said, taking a step away from him.

"So this is embarrassing. Looks like I might have interrupted something." Ali glanced from Ivey to him, and pierced him with her Big Sister look.

He and Ivey spoke at once.

"You didn't interrupt anything," Ivey said.

"Yes, you did."

"Mom and Dad are around here some-where. Have you seen them?" Ali continued, despite his do-you-want-to-die stare. The look had worked when he was fourteen and she had made it her mission to make sure he stayed on the straight and narrow—otherwise known as tattling—but the glare wasn't working for him now. He loved Ali, but he already had a mother.

"Nope, but I'll catch up with them later."

Ali turned to Ivey. "So what's this I saw on the news about your aunt's condo being repossessed? Wow, that's some excitement, huh? We don't get the FBI much in little ole Starlight Hill."

The unspoken message seemed to be: "leave it to you and your aunt to bring the FBI to town." It took great effort to remember that his sister was only looking out for him, and that she didn't want to see him hurt again. Without thinking, he reached for Ivey's hand and squeezed it. "This all has to do with Ben Cartwright, and making restitution to his investors. It has nothing to do with Ivey or her aunt."

Someone or something slammed into his knees, and he looked down to see Becky. Bob followed behind her, holding a sleeping Liam.

"Hey, squirt."

"Uncle Jeff! I saw a clown! He painted my face! And I have a balloon!" Becky babbled.

The kid was so filled with excitement he half expected her to levitate.

"She's had too much sugar," Ali said, by way of explanation.

"Becky, this is my friend, Ivey." Jeff introduced two of his favorite girls. Once Ali would have qualified too, except that right now he wanted to kill her.

"Hi! I'm four! How old are you?" Becky asked, reminding him of a spinning top.

"You don't ask grown-ups how old they are," Bob the Saint corrected with a sigh.

But Jeff couldn't help notice that Ivey smiled at Becky like she'd seen the sun set in gold, red, and orange. "That's okay. I'm old, too old to count."

"No, you're not!" Becky laughed, and climbed out of his arms. "My Grandma's old." She started running in the general direction of the street, Bob following quickly behind.

"I better go too," Ali said with a conciliatory look in her eyes. "Nice seeing you."

Jeff turned to Ivey when they'd left. "That's Ali's family. Becky isn't usually wound up like that. She's smart as a whip though."

"And adorable."

"Thanks. I am rather partial to her." Someday if he were lucky enough to have children, he hoped they'd challenge him as much as Becky did. She made him see things in new ways, in different colors and shapes. Ali said kids had a way of doing that.

He took Ivey's hand, and she went willingly with him away from the crowds and closer to the creek that ran in the back of the park. "I'm sorry about Ali. She's worried about me."

"Worried about you?" The tone in Ivey's voice suggested that she couldn't fathom a reason why Ali would worry about big, capable Jeff Garner. "Surely she knows you left me."

He cleared his throat. This was the hard part. Not the way he worked, but maybe it was time to make some changes. He would have to let his heart take the lead, because his brain was currently disengaged. "Yeah, of course she does. But here's the thing. She also knows what I haven't told you yet."

By the creek, a slight breeze kicked up and he instinctively pulled Ivey closer.

"What haven't you told me yet?" He

could feel it as her tiny frame tightened in expectation of another blow. Not surprising, since she'd lived her life recovering from a series of small shocks.

He let go of her and dragged a hand through his hair. "This isn't easy to say."

"Say it."

Right. "What you don't know is that after I said I needed a break I regretted it. Instead of calling you, I planned a surprise. You like surprises, I know that. Anyway, I asked for my grandmother's wedding ring, came home right after finals and picked it up. But you weren't home because you went to meet up with the guy you met on a dating service. And that's the truth."

Humiliating though it was, the truth felt liberating. And now he didn't feel like such an asshole. Yeah, maybe he'd made a selfish mistake, but he'd tried to correct it. He expected Ivey to be happy now, to know that he too had regrets. And that the joke had been on him.

But of all the things he expected, not one of them was to watch her burst into tears.

11

____

"Before I apologize, I need to know what I did wrong." Jeff pressed his forehead to hers.

The strong beat of his heart pulsed under her fingertips. With a slight push she turned away and faced the creek, trying hard to swallow a sob. "You did nothing wrong."

Every star winked back in the inky black night, but she had no words. No words for the unfairness of it all. For the irony. If she'd only waited one lousy month. She wouldn't have even been showing, so she would have had the pleasure of a proposal knowing it hadn't been born out of necessity. But beyond that, not much else would have been different.

He still might have had to drop out of school. They would have still wound up hating each other. No, she'd done the right thing.

She'd fixed it. Fixed everything. Only problem, she'd never had what she wanted. Maybe now it was finally her time.

Perhaps from this point forward she wouldn't cheat herself anymore. Stop making excuses and believing she didn't deserve to be happy. Tell the truth and let people deal with it. Take what she wanted, and try like hell to be happy. Life was too short.

And this man happened to be all she'd ever wanted from the moment she'd first laid eyes on him. Granted, most people didn't discover the love of their lives at sixteen, but she wasn't most people.

Neither was he for that matter. He happened to be—everything. And she deserved him.

Jeff came up behind her, his arms encircling her, head bent low to her neck. "Tell me you're okay."

She turned to face him. "I am, but we're going to have to set Ali straight."

"Don't worry about her." His thumb traced the edge of her eye, wiping away a tear.

"I have to worry about her. She's your sister, and she loves you. She's upset with me, and I get it. But she has to know that I'm not letting you go this time."

The furrowed brow eased and his face broke out in a smile. A surge of love kicked her in the gut so hard that it spread down and around to the back of her knees.

"Yeah?"

She rose to the tips of her toes to kiss him square on the lips, where she'd wanted to kiss him for weeks. He deepened the kiss, and she felt warmth as it spread down her legs, and to the soles of her feet. He tasted so good, warm and wet and hard under her touch. She let her hands wander down his back and then up his flat stomach, while his fingers threaded through her hair, holding her firmly in place. As if she would dream of going anywhere.

She pulled back, breathless and hazy but most of all certain. "Let's go."

They didn't bother saying goodbye to anyone as they left the park, and Jeff tugged on her hand like he thought if he didn't hurry she might change her mind.

Once at the cottage, when the door to the rest of the world closed and they were two lovers alone with their thoughts and their history, Jeff kissed the hollow of her throat and whispered near her ear. "Are you sure?"

She answered by leaping into his arms and wrapping her legs around his waist. Holding the back of his neck she kissed him hard, letting all the hurt, regret, anger, and pain slide right out of her body. "What do you think?"

He carried her to his bed and gently lowered her, his arms cradling her like she was something precious and breakable. She wanted to show him that she wasn't fragile any more. Instead she was strong and capable and ready to risk it all.

Eager, she fumbled to take her jeans off, fighting with a zipper that didn't understand how important this moment was to her. He'd once whispered that nothing turned him on quite as much as her eagerness for him, but he stayed her hand before she removed her black bra and panties.

"Slow down, Little Face." He ran his fingers under the satiny strap, and the warmth of his hand made her shiver.

"I don't know if I can."

"Me either, but I'm going to try," he said as he pulled her bra strap down and his mouth covered her breast.

In the back of her mind there was something she hadn't told him, but for now the uncomfortable truth faded to black because it was so much better to feel, to love, to touch him everywhere. The rest would take care of itself. She had to believe it.

Her eyes were closed, and she hadn't realized it until Jeff spoke. "Look at me."

And she did, taking it all in, the way he moved above her, causing her such pleasure she might jump out of her skin.

"I see you," she said on a sigh.

She saw everything she'd ever known about him and never forgotten. The way he knew how to love her, never judging her, seeing her heart even before she'd ever showed it to him.

As wave after wave of pleasure hit her,

there were no words left. Only sensations that carried her away.

~

Ivey sighed in Jeff's arms and snuggled in closer. This was bliss, lying in his arms. Feeling his heart beat next to hers. She hadn't wanted to admit it, but all that serial dating had amounted to the fact that there had never been anyone else for her except for Jeff Garner.

"I don't want to go anywhere else, ever again. Let's stay right here."

"Deal." Jeff ran his hand along the small of her back, and she settled in to the fact that his hands were not going to stop touching her for the foreseeable future. A little bit like heaven. "Maybe we should sleep for a while. I don't want to tire you out. The first time we were both a bit carried away, and it was too quick for me, but the second time felt more like we were getting reacquainted. And the third time we tried something new."

She felt a blush coming on. "I liked that."

"I could tell." He kissed her forehead.

"We may get into the swing of this the fourth time."

"But first I need to rest. For a little while." Ivey laid her head on his chest, listening to his strong and steady heartbeat. She'd missed this—him—so much that fears clouded her vision. She could lose him, because she had once before. He'd told her his secret. Now could she tell him hers? Would he still want her after that?

Yes he would. He wanted to marry you, remember? If he still didn't feel that way, would he have told her at all?

Her cell phone rang and Jeff groaned. She reached for it, but it was closer to him so he grabbed it first.

He playfully held it out of her reach. "Give me. It might be important. Remember I'm covering for Marissa this weekend."

"What will you give me for it?" He had a wicked smile on his face.

"I think you know what I'll give you." Ivey let her hand dive under the covers and he jumped.

"You've got a deal," he said as he handed her the phone.

When Ivey answered she heard a moan

on the other end. So either someone was having sex or about to have a baby. "This is Ivey. Hello?"

"It's Asia. Foster. Ow! Oh, mother of God that hurts. Are you going to help me or what?" Asia sounded pushy and in pain.

"Of course I will," Ivey said as she swatted Jeff's hand away from her breast. "What's going on?"

"I'm having a baby, Einstein. Are you sure you're qualified to do this?"

All right, so maybe Asia was a little bitchy as well. "How far apart are the contractions?"

"That's the thing. There's no pattern. Eleven minutes, seven minutes, eight minutes, twelve. What should I do? It's not like it says in the book!"

Ivey jumped out of bed and collected clothes from the floor. How had Asia done this? She was about to have a baby on the day she'd planned. It was one wild coincidence. "It's enough of a pattern. I'll be over in a few minutes. Don't worry. We still have plenty of time."

"You have to go," Jeff said when she hung up.

For the first time since she'd been doing this, she'd rather stay home than go deliver a baby into the world. That might be because Jeff lay on his back, arms splayed behind his neck, only the thinnest of sheets covering him. Especially difficult, because she was well acquainted with what lay under the sheet.

"Lousy timing, but babies have their own schedule."

"So I've heard."

"I'll make this up to you." She leaned down and gave him a long, deep kiss.

He grinned. "You better."

ONE QUICK SHOWER LATER, which Jeff couldn't talk Ivey into sharing with him, and she was off. Now he stood alone in the kitchen, fully dressed but not happy about it, heating up a can of chicken soup. It took him a few minutes to realize he was whistling. *Whistling.*

A couple of uninterrupted hours with Ivey had done that. At first he hadn't known what to expect, being together after all these years, but it was better than he could have imagined. Better than his oldest fantasies. He hadn't been a monk all these years, but he had cheated himself. There was nothing quite like sex with someone you loved, and he'd done that for the first time in years tonight.

She remembered him. The way he liked to be touched, everything he'd taught her about how to please him. And she'd done that tonight, with the kind of passion he remembered. Ivey wasn't shy or retiring with him, she was eager and took what she wanted. This had to be love, the kind that didn't fade away, and from now on he wasn't going to settle for anything less.

If it meant he had to make more sacrifices, give up more of himself, lose sleep, he'd do it. He didn't know how Ivey felt, but he'd find out soon enough. This time, he wasn't going to let her walk away without an explanation.

There was a short, insistent knock on the door, and Jeff halfway convinced himself that Ivey was back, having forgotten her key. Instead an older woman stood in front of him, dressed in a peasant top, jeans, and Birkenstocks.

"I heard from my friend Marissa that Ivey Lancaster is living here. Is she here now?"

"Sorry no, she's with a patient."

"Don't tell me at the hospital."

"She's covering for a midwife who's out of town. It's going to be a while, I think." He hoped the woman would get the message. She should come back later.

"Fine. I'll wait for her if you don't mind. I'm up from LA, trying to talk her into letting go of this foolishness with the hospital. I heard all about it from Marissa. Ivey and I used to work together."

Jeff moved aside and waved the woman inside. Apparently he would have company for a while. "You must be Babs. She's talked about you."

Babs took a seat on the couch, and for the first time he noticed the overnight bag. Great. Did she think she would stay the night here? He stared at the bag, trying to mentally telegraph that she wasn't going to be able to. On the other hand, Babs could have Scott's room and Ivey could stay with him. Face it, as far as he was concerned, she'd never sleep in Scott's room again.

"Ivey and I go way back. Never would have thought I'd mentor one of my own patients, but Ivey was special."

He froze. "Excuse me?"

"I said she was special."

"You said she was one of your patients. Maybe I heard wrong." Wouldn't she have told him if she'd been pregnant? They'd been discussing labor and delivery for weeks, and she never thought to add her own personal experience? Why hide that from him? Did she think he of all people would judge her? Or — the other thought that immediately ran through his mind was too terrible to be true.

Bab's eyes narrowed. "Wait a minute. What did you say your name was again?"

"I didn't. How long ago was she your patient?"

Now she looked nervous, and Jeff could feel anger roiling around in the pit of his stomach. But it couldn't be true. Ivey wouldn't have done this to him.

"I think you should talk to Ivey," she said

with a mortified look that gave him his answer.

But it was much too late for her to stop talking now. He forced himself to speak calmly. "Answer the question. How long ago? A year ago? Five years ago? When?"

Babs sighed and looked directly in his eyes. "I'm not going to say anymore, but you're asking the right questions. Ivey was my patient five years ago."

His baby? How did he miss it? Five years ago, Ivey had been suddenly clingy and tearful. Out of the blue she'd asked him about family housing for married students. He'd only felt the noose tighten around his neck and made up some lame excuse about it being too crowded. Too expensive. Too late to sign up. He'd wanted her to be patient. It was going to be bad enough being married on a resident's salary, but he couldn't stand the thought of having his wife work to put him through school. No, waiting and planning was best.

Obviously he hadn't had all the facts. Ivey had been pregnant with his baby. Didn't think he had a right to know. Phased him out, just like that.

Jeff had never felt hot molten lava course through his veins before, but damn if there wasn't a first time for everything. "I have to go. Stay here as long as you like."

"Wait. Where are you going?" The woman wouldn't stop talking, but he could barely hear her words, little bites of sound in the distance.

Suddenly the past had ringing clarity to it, even as red seemed to cloud his vision.

His fingers tightened around the steering wheel, and he hit the dashboard with his fist. So many questions to be answered from the one woman who couldn't seem to stop hurting him. This one final dig, taking his child away, was almost more than he could take.

He didn't care that he'd be interrupting, as he drove to the Foster house. He didn't care anymore because he needed answers and he wasn't going to wait another second for them.

12

It might be a long night with little sleep for any of them, but at the end of it Asia would hold her baby in her arms for the first time. Ivey still wasn't sure how Asia had managed to nail her delivery date so accurately. Call it luck or good timing, but the Fosters seemed to have both in spades.

"You're sixty percent effaced and two centimeters dilated." Ivey took her gloves off.

"Two? Only two? Tell me why I feel like I'm at twenty."

"Honey, it's okay." Asia's husband Derek massaged her back.

"Don't touch me."

Derek looked wounded, and Ivey gave

him a little apologetic smile. "Prodromal labor is hard, but you'll get there. You probably have a big baby, and he or she is tiring your poor womb out. But this is going to happen soon. We need to wait the baby out. So far everything looks great."

"You'll stay with us. Right?" Derek asked, the high pitch in his voice and the terror in his eyes giving her a clear idea of his level of apprehension. She'd give him a ten, ninety-nine percent effaced. Poor guy.

"I'm not going anywhere. Why don't you get her some more ice chips?"

Derek, given a green light to do something away from his wife, took off at a near run.

"Remind me why I did this," Asia said. "Why have his baby? He's so damn big, no wonder his baby is big. Why couldn't I have fallen in love with someone smaller? Thinner?"

Glad Derek was out of the room, Ivey wiped Asia's face with a soft, damp towel. "Because you love him?"

"Oh, God help me, I do." Asia sobbed. "I was so mean to him. Derek! Come back here. I didn't mean it. I love you, baby."

Derek didn't waste any time hightailing back into the room with the ice chips, the look of a happy puppy dog in his eyes. "You called me, baby?"

Ivey left the bedroom, giving them a moment. This was the best part of a home birth. *Home.* She'd be in the kitchen if they needed her. In a few minutes, she'd be back to suggest that Asia take a walk and move around some more. Meanwhile, time was their best friend.

But it wouldn't be the same in a hospital setting, even if the women's center had birthing rooms they'd designed to look like bedrooms. It wasn't home, and Ivey could see Marissa's point.

Being an employee of the hospital would mean that Ivey would be used for more than one function and maybe more than one patient at a time. It was in the economy of health care. Time spent waiting for nature to take its course might not fit into the natural ebb and flow of the hospital.

From the kitchen window, Ivey saw the bright headlights of a car pull up the driveway. The Fosters were private people, and they hadn't invited any extended family to the event. They weren't expecting anyone.

Ivey made her way to the front door to discourage any eager friends or relatives from coming any further when she noticed Jeff. One look at him, his purposeful stride towards the house, and she realized something had changed. It was in the set of his jaw and in the way he held himself like a tightly wound cord. In an instant she knew.

She rushed to meet him on the front lawn of the home. They couldn't do this. Not here, not now. She needed a minute, or another month. Another year. She wasn't ready, even after all this time.

"We need to talk," Jeff said.

"Now's not a good time."

"Then make it a good time, because this isn't going to wait."

"It has to wait. I have a patient—"

"What did you do with my child?" He took another step toward Ivey, the heat of his anger nearly emanating off of him in waves.

Oh, not this. She'd wanted to spare him all along. Maybe she'd been selfish, or maybe she'd been selfless. Either way, Jeff was about to hurt in places he didn't even know existed and all because of her.

"Answer me!"

The emotion she heard in his voice mixed in with the anger turned her answer into a strangled sob. "There *is* no child. I had a miscarriage."

He flinched like he'd been slapped, and his body seemed to cave in a little at that answer. "Why?"

She realized that he wasn't asking why she'd lost the baby. It was a bigger why. He wanted to know why she'd never told him.

"You didn't want me anymore. If I told you, I knew you would have done the right thing. You would have married me, and you didn't want to get married. Not then. I have enough pride to want to be married because someone loves me and not out of obligation."

"So this was all about you? No—you made a decision for both of us. And you didn't have the right to do that."

Those words were like bullets hitting her heart. Yeah, she had no right, but she'd done it anyway. "You wouldn't be a doctor today. You might have had to drop out of school."

"So you did it for me?" The tone in his

voice left no doubt that he didn't believe her for a second.

"For you and for me. I was going to tell you someday."

The words sounded so empty. So false. Because they'd been the words and thoughts of a scared and stubborn twenty-year-old who didn't know any better. Who wouldn't listen to what anyone else told her.

"Some. Day."

"If I'd given birth, I would have told you. Eventually. I would have let you be a part of our baby's life."

He slashed a hand through his hair. "Would you? That's really big of you."

He moved another step toward her, closing the distance between them.

"Look, I get that you're mad. But this is not the time or the—"

"Mad? Ivey, what you did went so far over the line that the line is a dot in the distance."

"But—I did it for you. You had our lives planned out, and the baby didn't fit in." Why couldn't he see the noble sacrifice she'd made so that he could finish school without complications? What about that?

"We made love tonight. What if you'd

gotten pregnant? Would you tell me this time or would you walk away again?"

"That's not fair. Of course I wouldn't. It's different."

"What's different? I loved you then, and I love you now. I don't care about any of the details. We would have worked it out."

With one swift move his right hand pulled her forehead to his own and held it tightly in place. She felt the strength of his anger, barely restrained and bubbling beneath the surface. But it was the tears forming in his eyes that caused another sob to hitch in her throat.

"I'm sorry."

"You. Had. No. Right."

He released her and stomped back to his car, taking off without another look in her direction. She stayed rooted to the spot on the Foster's lawn, right near the azalea bush. Wondering as she watched Jeff drive off if those were the last words he'd ever say to her.

Turned out that no one thought having their choice taken away was any kind of favor. Jeff included. She ought to know that better than anyone. Wasn't she fighting so that women could have more choices in a hospital setting? And yet she hadn't given Jeff the same respect.

It dawned on her how much she'd hurt him.

"Miss Ivey?" It was Derek, calling out to her from inside the screened front door. "You okay?"

Ivey kept her back to him as she wiped the tears away, and squared her shoulders. "I'm fine."

"I thought I heard shouting."

She turned to see the concerned look of a Daddy-to-be, already in full-fledged protective mode. He'd be a good dad.

Like Jeff would have been.

And suddenly Ivey couldn't breathe. Maybe this was why she hadn't wanted to come home for so long. Why she'd stayed away. She'd already lost enough, hurt enough, and cried enough.

But not with him.

The only person who'd ever said anything that made any sense was Babs, who after the miscarriage had told Ivey that no one but the baby's father would fully understand her grief. But she hadn't shared that with him. She hadn't shared her grief with anyone.

Everything had been all right while she pretended, while she kept the truth locked away safely in her heart.

"Miss Ivey?" Derek stood at the door, and it didn't look like he'd be going back inside anytime soon.

Ivey swallowed back a sob. "It was a big misunderstanding."

The width and span of which might be too great to ever get over.

JEFF DROVE because he had to keep moving. If he didn't move, he would have to hit something. Hard. He had to get away from Ivey, because he was too angry to talk any more. Too hurt to try to understand. Like a lighthouse to a ship, the hospital beckoned. The best thing to do after a shocking, life-changing event had to be something normal. Routine. That's what he needed right now.

And he still wanted to check on Frank. When he'd dropped by earlier in the day, Frank had been out of his room for more tests. Jeff still wanted to know what he'd missed. In the ER he'd run every test he could think of and come up with nothing. Somehow, though, he'd missed it. Frank had a heart condition.

He took the elevator up to the cardiac wing of the hospital and asked the night shift nurse for Frank's room number. By now he was under the care of a specialist, and maybe Dr. Bryans would have some answers.

Jeff ran into Dr. Bryans in the hallway. "How's Frank Sullivan? I came to check on him."

"He'll be fine. Thanks to all those tests you ran on him, I had a basis of comparison. He's healthy for the most part, but his heart shows some cardiomyopathy, probably from the undiagnosed arrhythmia. Never caught it on the EKG, so it's probably paroxysmal. Something his regular doctor should have caught with a twenty-four hour Holter monitor."

"He didn't seem to have a regular doctor." Something Jeff should have pressed Frank on. Should have demanded to talk to someone at the assisted living center or a relative and make sure they followed up.

"Yeah, that's what he told me." Bryans grabbed the elevator. "Not to worry. He'll be fine."

Jeff wasn't fine though. He'd had Frank in the ER for a few hours at a time, sometimes several times a week, and he'd still missed it. Sometimes if you turned your head for a second you could miss so much.

More and more it appeared emergency medicine wasn't for him. He wanted, needed, to be more involved in the outcome.

Ivey had denied him that, but no one else would ever again. He should have been there for her, in those days when she would have been scared and alone. When he might have made a difference. Or not.

But at least he would have been there for her, for their baby. She hadn't given him that chance, maybe because she didn't trust him enough. Couldn't trust that he'd take care of her, because no else ever had. And she didn't believe he loved her. Not enough.

And whose fault is that, idiot?

Jeff sat on an empty chair beside Frank's bed for several minutes until the man's eyes fluttered open.

"Well, hot damn. My favorite doctor."

"Thought you might want to see what I look like without a stethoscope around my neck."

"No bags under the eyes, either. Doc, have you been relaxing?"

"Something like that." He supposed he'd been happy, for about a nanosecond. And Ivey had something to do with it, like as she had everything to do with his misery now. "I did have a couple days off."

"Just what I ordered." Frank winked.

"You're going to be okay," Jeff reassured him. "Now that we know what's wrong, we can fix it."

"What about you? Can we fix what's wrong with you?"

"I'm fine," Jeff closed his eyes and pinched the bridge of his nose. Or he would be anyway. Someday.

"If you say so, Doc. But if I promise not to come to the ER any more, will you promise you won't always be here? I'd like to think of you, young as you are, enjoying life."

"Why? Work is a good thing." It was all he would have now, and maybe all he'd ever need.

He'd see about switching specialties

soon, maybe cardiology or pediatrics. Something in which he could be around for the duration. Witness the outcome. He'd have to start over again but that was okay. Ivey had done it, and so could he.

"Work is great, it's just not enough. No lie, trust me, it'll never be enough."

Jeff didn't believe him. For years now, medicine had been front-and-center in his life and he hadn't questioned it. Not until Ivey had come back to town and sent his heart and hormones into overdrive. "Let's talk about you. Do you have any family? Someone who can be here with you?"

"I have kids, but I hate to bother them."

"How many?"

"Six." Frank grinned. "I was a busy man in my youth, Doc."

"Yes, you were. I'm sure they'd want to know what's going on with you. Did someone call them?"

"I have my oldest son on the contact list. He's flying out from Utah." Frank sighed. "He won't be happy."

"I'm sure he's worried."

"It's not that. He works all the time. Anyway, I can't complain because his salary pays for the prison—I mean the assisted living center. Because you know, I'm too old to remember how to turn off a stove. Might burn the place down." Frank rolled his eyes.

They continued to talk about Frank's family and kids for several minutes. It turned out Frank was a widower, and he still got teary mentioning his wife's name. After about half an hour, Frank's eyes were at half-mast, and Jeff decided he'd tired him out enough.

"Rest. I'm glad you're going to be okay." Jeff patted his arm and rose to leave.

On his way to the parking lot, he saw Lillian leaving. She caught up to Jeff, and they walked out to the lot together.

"Thanks to your and Ivey's recommendation, the board agreed to hire one midwife to start the trial. We'll see how it goes from there. I want to thank you. You had an open mind, and I appreciate that."

"Thank Ivey. She's persuasive when she wants to be." And a good liar too.

"Do you think she's still interested in the position?"

"You should call her."

"I will. I don't want to lose her." Lillian waved as they parted ways.

He hadn't wanted to lose her either, but it seemed inevitable now. He'd lost her a long time ago.

He couldn't go home, so he drove out of town and back again. Then wound up where he should have all along.

Ali opened the front door. "Providence. That's what this is. Pure and simple providence. Bob is working late and Becky won't go to sleep. Here, you take Liam, and I'll go in and hold her down till she falls asleep."

He must have given her a weird look, because she shook her head. "I'm not really going to hold her down."

"I didn't think so, Ali."

He carried Liam to the couch, plopped him down, and sat next to him. Liam was two and didn't like Jeff much. Or at least it always felt that way, because Liam didn't say a peep around Jeff, and word out on the street was that Liam had learned to talk. Jeff and Becky were pals, but for Liam, it seemed like the jury was still out. Jeff couldn't blame the kid since they didn't see each other often enough.

Liam, pacifier firmly stuck in his mouth, scrambled off the couch and handed him items from the coffee table. The remote control, a deck of cards, every single coaster on the table. Was he supposed to hold everything the kid gave him? Jeff set them back on the table, but Liam handed everything back to him. The kid was on some kind of mission to unclutter the coffee table.

Finally he picked up a magazine—*Ladies' Home Journal*—handed it to Jeff and climbed in his lap, where he proceeded to flip each page with the finesse of an orangutan.

"Don't worry, kid. You'll get those fine motor skills."

Liam looked up at him, as if he questioned Jeff's sanity.

When Jeff started reading the Oil of Olay ad out loud to pass the time, Liam actually snuggled up to listen.

"Erases fine lines and wrinkles." He kept reading, and Liam kept getting limper in his arms. So this was the secret. Bore them to sleep.

Kids weren't so difficult. He didn't know what Ali was always whining about. Liam's soft blonde hair brushed against Jeff's chin and the smell of Johnson's Baby Shampoo brought back a childhood memory.

He wondered if he and Ivey would have had a boy or a girl. Whether it would have hurt any less to know when she'd miscarried, instead of being blindsided now.

"Bless you. He's asleep. How'd you do it?" Ali whispered, lifting Liam out of his arms.

"Oil of Olay."

Ali made a face. "I never understand your jokes."

The story of his life. When Ali came back, she had a glass of wine in each hand.

Now it was his turn to be grateful as she handed him the glass of chilled white wine.

"Chardonnay, Clos La Chance 2011," Ali said, because she fancied herself a wine connoisseur. "It's not bad. To what do I owe this unexpected visit? Did they finally decide to give you a day off?"

"Something like that."

"Well, why don't you look happier? Wait. Let me take a wild guess. Ivey."

"You have no idea." And then, because Ali was his big sister and he didn't currently owe Ivey a lick of loyalty, he told Ali everything.

She didn't speak for a moment. Maybe she was also thinking about the fact that in a different outcome, he'd have a child Becky's age. Then Ali's eyes watered, which made his stomach clench some more. "I'm so sorry. What a lousy way to find out."

"Why didn't she tell me? Maybe you can do me the favor of explaining womankind to me. You are my sister, and I did let you have my ice cream cone that one time you dropped yours because you're such a damn klutz."

Ali rolled her eyes. "I can't explain womankind to you, because even I don't always understand women. We're all different, and contrary to what you men think, there's no secret handshake. You and I both know that Ivey had a lifetime of keeping secrets, protecting those she loved. It doesn't seem like such a stretch to think she'd try to protect you too. Yeah, it was lousy and it was wrong, but the truth is I kind of understand."

"I can't believe you're defending her."

"I'm not defending her. I hate what she did. But I said I understand why she did it."

"She didn't have to do me any favors. Didn't she think I could handle being a father? Is that how little she thinks of me?" He heard the sound of his own voice, sounding like a stranger's. Angry. Bitter. Hurt.

"Shhhh, you'll wake the kids. You're going to make a great father someday, weird jokes aside. But you weren't ready to be a father back then. Think about it. I actually recall you saying the words 'I'm dying here.' You didn't have time to come home for the weekend, what makes you think you had time to be a father?"

"Ouch." Ali had a way of cutting to the heart of the matter.

"I'm not kidding. This is my life." She waved a hand, spanning the room. "I'm deliriously happy to be having a glass of wine at nine o'clock and some grown-up conversation. Do you know what I found the other day? Do you?"

"I have a feeling I don't."

Ali got closer, ruffling her hair and pointing to her scalp. "There! See that? Can you believe it?"

Ali had always been a bit dramatic. Mom was right about that, come to think of it. "I don't see anything but hair. What am I looking for?"

"My first gray hair! Can't you see it?" Ali continued pointing to her scalp.

"One gray hair? How am I supposed to find it?"

"I'm thirty-two years old and I have my first gray hair. Found it right after Liam was born." She sat back down on the couch, smoothing her short brown hair back into place. "That is what kids will do to you."

"I don't care about gray hair."

"See, you would have as a medical student with a wife and child. You probably would have a full head of gray hair when all was said and done."

He was about to say that it worked for George Clooney, but he was beginning to see Ali's point.

Ali turned to him with that annoying superior-big-sister look she'd spent years refining. "Not to mention you and Ivey would have wound up hating each other."

He scoffed. "Ironic, since we're not together now."

"Yeah, sure. Like I believe that. Do you know how many young marriages end in divorce? What's the divorce rate for doctors?"

"Okay, okay, I get it. I wasn't ready back

then, but I'll never believe that I didn't have the right to know. To be involved. It was my baby too."

Ali nodded. "So what are you going to do?"

"I don't know. The problem is I think I still love her."

"Shocking," Ali said. "I called it. Like magnets."

"But I can't trust her." He pulled out his phone. It had been buzzing on and off for the past couple of hours, and he'd been ignoring it on purpose. The hospital would page him, and he wasn't even on call. He had a good feeling who had been calling him, and it didn't surprise him when he finally took a look.

Several missed calls from Ivey. And two text messages: *You don't understand. Please let me explain.*

Maybe it was time to listen.

13

———————

When Ivey returned the following morning, she hadn't expected to find Babs napping on the couch in the family room. Ivey stifled the groan that formed in her throat. She wouldn't have to ask Jeff how he found out.

Babs sat up, rubbed her eyes and stretched. "What is wrong with you young people? I visit, and that man leaves me here alone. For hours! What if I was a thief or worse, an ax murderer? Where's his sense of safety?"

"What are you doing here?"

"Marissa called me, and I needed to see you in person. This is important." Babs stood and smoothed down her rumpled jeans. "But first, I'm afraid I spoke out of turn earlier."

"I know. And your timing is horrible."

"Well, I'm sorry about that. I didn't tell him much, but he guessed. Anyway, I know about the women's center, and I've come here to give you my opinion in person."

So Marissa had called in reinforcements. But Ivey had already made up her mind, especially after last night. "I don't need your opinion. I've already made my decision."

"Good. I was worried after Marissa called and told me."

"I'm going to do it." Baby boy Foster had been born early this morning on the same bed where his parents likely conceived him, bathed by the soft light of his mother's reading lamp, while his father wept (he couldn't read the poem after all). Ivey didn't think a hospital could replicate that in a hundred years.

Not without her there to help them.

"Didn't I teach you better than this? Doctors don't understand birth. Even women doctors. I don't know what they do to them in medical school, but you'd think that labor and delivery were something they have to cure."

"Look, I understand. Believe me. Tonight Asia Foster gave birth at home, and it was beautiful. I wish every woman would do that. But the truth is they're not. For whatever reason, they're going to feel safer in a hospital setting. I know it's not the easy thing to do, and I'm sorry if I'm letting you down. Jeff and I turned in our recommendation to the board. And if they'll have me, I'm going to work at the women's center. I want to make sure that every woman can have the childbirth experience they want."

"But the doctors aren't going to let them have that experience!"

"Well that's exactly why they need me there."

"You're one tiny girl, up against territorial doctors who are going to defend their livelihood to the death."

"Let them. I'm fiercer than I look, and you ought to know that."

Babs' gray eyes softened. "I still remember the young girl who came to me pregnant with her first child, wanting to have that perfect birth. You'd read everything you could get your hands on and already knew what you wanted."

"I didn't get very far." Ivey's breath hitched, for one minute drawn back to that time when she thought for a few months that she'd been blessed. Finally, she must have done something right. She'd failed to take care of Mama, because she hadn't been able to stop her from driving off the road. Failed to plan ahead, like so many times before. But this time, she wouldn't fail.

Only she had. Even eating the healthiest diet, taking her vitamins, doing everything she'd been asked to do and then some, she'd lost the best mistake she ever made.

Babs gathered Ivey in her arms. "You never get over losing a baby, honey. I tried to tell you that, even as you wanted to act like delivering someone else's babies would somehow make up for the fact that you never got to have your own precious child."

Is that what she'd done? "I thought it was all in the past as long as I didn't think about it. But when I came back home, when I saw him . . ."

"It all came back, didn't it?"

Not while she could pretend for a while

that it had never happened. Jeff didn't know, after all. Except that now he did, and she was somehow reliving the hurt all over again.

The memories—bleeding and in agonizing pain, rushing to the hospital. Babs had met her there and tried to be a friend because the client-midwife relationship was over. Aunt Lucy had come to see Ivey a few days later, insisting that it was all for the best and that someday she could try again. Saying all the wrong things, even with the best of intentions. But the pregnancy hadn't been an inconvenience to her. It had been her baby.

Like so many good things in her life, the joy hadn't lasted. Didn't have staying power. "I wasn't ready to tell him."

"It's good that he knows. You need someone to grieve your loss with you as only he can do."

Like he'd been summoned, Jeff chose that moment to walk through the front door.

Babs stared from him to Ivey, then back again. "I'll leave you two alone."

Ivey didn't even say goodbye, because her eyes were riveted on Jeff, who looked like he wanted to say a million things or maybe nothing at all.

He held the door open for Babs, nodded to her as she left, and shut the door again.

"Where were you?" It was the only thing she could think to ask him. Not "will you ever forgive me," or "can't you at least try and understand?"

"Driving, mostly. I stopped by the hospital, and I stopped by Ali's. And then I kept driving until I thought I could be calm enough to listen to you." He scrubbed a hand across his face, and from the looks of it, he still hadn't yet reached that point.

"You have to understand—"

"I don't have to do anything, Ivey." His jaw quivered almost imperceptibly, but she noticed it.

"Okay, you don't have to. But if you would try to imagine how I felt—"

"What do you think I've been doing for the past few hours? Over and over in my mind I've thought about how scared you must have been. What it must have felt like to lose our baby. All the physical pain you went through. And all I can think is that I should have been there, but because of you I wasn't. You didn't trust me enough. Didn't think I could handle it."

"No, it's not that," she protested. "I didn't want you to feel obligated. I didn't want to ruin your plans for the future."

"Screw planning. Maybe I needed something to show me that the best things in life just happen. You didn't give me a choice. You lied to me. I've never lied to you."

"I know I was wrong. But can't you forgive me?" She moved closer to him, but he was a hard, solid wall of anger.

And he didn't answer for a few lonely seconds. "I don't know."

The answer made the tight fist of fear in her stomach open up and spread to the tips of her toes.

Ivey fingered the soft bristles on his jawline and tucked a lock of his hair that had fallen over his eye. "I love you, and you love me. We can get past this." *Please, God, let us get past this.* She'd never wanted anything more in her life. Another chance. Did anyone really get over their first love? She never had.

His eyes were wet, and she thought maybe she really would die right here and now because she'd done this. She'd caused him this pain.

He took her hand and kissed the back of it. "I don't know. I need some time."

Time. Right. Time away from her. She was familiar with that refrain. "Maybe I should go stay with Brooke."

This was where he would protest, and let her stay here where maybe within the next day or so they'd be back in each other's arms again. But he only gazed at her with red-rimmed eyes and said, "Maybe you should."

IVEY AND BROOKE hadn't tripped over each other yet, but they had bumped into each other several times over the past week. Hard not to in a nine-hundred-square-foot cottage.

Even so, Brooke wouldn't hear of any other arrangement.

"This is temporary, because you two will be back together in no time," Brooke said as they stood hip to hip in what passed as the kitchen.

"Don't be so sure. You might be stuck with me, and rentals don't come up every day."

"You're telling me. I've wanted to get out

of this place for years. I've got enough money saved up and no place to rent. But I've got my eye on Mrs. McCreety's place. She's ninety. How much longer can she last?"

"Brooke!" Was that what it had come to? Wishing people dead?

Brooke only shrugged. "The thing to do is buy land. One of these days I'll get my hands on some of it."

Everybody had to have a dream. Ivey had received part of her dream a few days ago when Lillian phoned with the job offer. She'd start next month, working in the women's center. One of her proudest achievements, and she wasn't sure why it didn't feel like enough.

Now, the tears—she'd shed enough of those. It had been a week of staying in, feeling sorry for herself, and waiting for a phone call. But she was all done with pathetic and ready at the very least to go to lunch and maybe for a little retail therapy.

Brooke drove, since she had a nice BMW company car and Ivey had still to go car shopping. Brooke cruised down Main Street. For a Saturday in the middle of the day, it wasn't all that busy. Then again the grape harvest had come and gone, and summer and tourist season were about to close up shop.

"Where to?" Brooke asked. "Anywhere. It's my treat."

"Anywhere but Mama's Diner." Ivey might run into Jeff there, and she wasn't ready. She'd need to be ready by next month when she started her job at the hospital, but by then, well, she didn't know what she would do, but she'd figure something out.

"Let's try Sweet Southern Buns. It's brand new and I haven't tried it yet."

Ivey didn't notice the ribbon until they were at the front door to the eatery. But right there, poised prominently on the front door —a beautiful and large pink ribbon. Clearly new and fresh, not an old faded one from the past.

"Oh no," Ivey breathed, but Brooke pretty much pushed through the front door.

"Don't worry, I'll find out what this is all about," Brooke said, waving to a petite young redhead.

"Hi, Brooke. I ordered my pink ribbon as soon as I heard. And you must be Ivey. I'm Genevieve, and I own this place. Bought it from Mrs. Lewis." She waved a hand around the small bakery filled with porcelain, teacups, and pictures of Paris on the walls.

"Why do you have a pink ribbon?" Ivey managed to squeak out.

"I heard you two broke up again and the chamber decided to go back to the ribbons. It's the best way of letting everyone know which side we represent."

"Sides? There are no sides," Ivey said as she took a seat at one of the wrought-iron tables.

"It's fun. Don't you love small towns and all their little quirks?"

"No," Brooke answered.

"Remind me again why I decided to go out today." Ivey threw a pointed look at Brooke.

"To show your face. Let everyone know 'Hello world, it's me, Ivey, and I'm not going to go down without a fight.' Something like that, anyway."

"Oh yeah. I forgot." Ivey tried to break out a smile and it took such effort she was sure it died before it even got to her lips. Not happening today.

Brooke noticed. "See that? That's exactly why I'm never falling in love."

"What?"

"That look on your face. Love hurts. And you've let love for that man torture you since you were sixteen years old."

"I should have told him."

"All right, so maybe I was wrong. Next time don't take advice from a woman who's never been in a serious and committed relationship. I can't do much more for you, but I promise you I'll take care of those pink and blue ribbons."

"I don't mind, actually. It's kind of sweet."

"How is it sweet?"

"They do it because they care about us. They're showing their support the only way they know how. And Genevieve is right. It is kind of fun. All the blue and pink ribbons all over town. Like a party."

"That's a new way to look at it. I remember how upset you were when you first heard about it."

But when she'd first come home, she'd tried to move forward and pretend she hadn't lost everything. She'd always felt like the wronged one, but it turned out that hadn't been entirely true.

Seemed also that she was stronger than ribbons.

After lunch, Brooke and Ivey walked past storefronts covered in pink and blue ribbons. For the first time, Ivey noticed many storefronts with both a pink and a blue ribbon and people who were smiling and winking. This, she supposed, passed for entertainment. No harm done.

They heard the loud voice of a woman inside Ed's Hardware store. "Seriously, get a hobby. Get a life. Stop giving these out!"

"Give those back to me. They're for paying customers!" Ed could be heard shouting back.

"Send me the bill." Ivey nearly collided with Ali as she stormed out the front door, carrying a box of blue ribbons. "Sorry about all this. I know how it must seem."

"I don't mind anymore," Ivey explained. But she couldn't stop staring at the box of blue ribbons in Ali's hands.

"We've decided it's quaint," Brooke offered.

Ali smiled. "Is quaint the new word for crazy?"

All three of them had a good laugh, while Ed eyed them suspiciously through the front glass door entrance.

Ali pulled Ivey to the side. "But seriously, please don't give up on him. I happen to know that he loves you."

"I know. And I love him." She would until the day she died, but maybe love wasn't enough when two people had hurt each other so much.

"He's super stubborn when he's hurt. He usually nurses his wounds for a while, like a grumpy bear. And I know work has been strangling him from the inside out for some time. Please be patient."

"All right," Ivey said with a shaky voice.

Ali waved good-bye, throwing the box of ribbons in the trunk of her car and slamming it shut with a loud thump.

"Wow. That was something, huh?" Brooke asked.

Amazing, seeing Ali come to Ivey's defense that way. Ivey would have expected even worse from her, once she'd found out about the big lie. Not this kind of compassion and understanding from the woman who would have done anything to protect Jeff.

Unless she was finally clear on the fact that he didn't need any protecting from Ivey.

14

"Are you certain?" Dr. Cooper asked.

"I haven't come to the decision lightly. I'm sure." Jeff sat across from the chief of cardiology.

"I know how hard you've worked for the hospital. If I'm being honest, I'd love for you to come on board."

No, it hadn't been part of the plan, but there it was. Emergency medicine wasn't a good fit, and the more Jeff had considered it over the past two weeks, cardiology fit right with where he wanted and needed to be. He didn't want to wind up four years later, unhappy with his career, still questioning whether or not he was doing any good. And was there anything more important to the human condition than the heart?

"And a pediatric cardiologist? Dr. Leonard is doing great work here. He'll be thrilled."

"I guess it's a matter of waiting for an opening now. I've already informed my attending."

"Right. I'll meet with Lillian, and we'll see how fast we can get this done."

Jeff made his way to the lounge and his locker. He wasn't kidding himself. It might be a while before there was a resident slot in cardiology. But now that he was certain of where he needed to be, he didn't mind waiting.

He still had a lot on his plate for today. Okay maybe he was still a little bit into planning, but who would have thought he'd wind up pursuing a specialty in pediatrics? Still, the more he'd thought about it the better it felt. Seemed right, rang true to him. He'd always liked kids, had once planned to have three of them with Ivey's help. And in some small way, he thought maybe if he could help sick kids, he'd be making up for the fact that he hadn't been there for his own baby.

Yeah, it hadn't been his fault. Not entirely. But maybe if he hadn't been so insistent on planning every aspect of their future life together, Ivey might have felt comfortable coming to him. She might not have thought she'd be ruining everything. Maybe if he hadn't been so wrapped up in medicine, in his career, expecting Ivey to meekly come along as a silent partner, he would have seen the signs.

Some things in life did require planning. Only not when it came to love. He hadn't expected to fall in love in high school. Certainly hadn't thought he'd want to marry his first love. But that's exactly what would happen, if Ivey would still have him. Because he couldn't be without her. Not like he hadn't tried. They both had. Five years and she wasn't out of his system. When she'd waltzed back into town, something in his heart popped open, and it was almost as if his life had been on pause for five years. Then Ivey had hit "play" again and they'd been off to the races.

He was a long way from being able to support a wife in the style he'd planned at one time, and he had a few years ahead of him before he could be in practice. But he'd leave it up to Ivey this time. They didn't have to wait another minute to be married as far as he was concerned. There was an official courthouse in the next town over, and if that didn't work, there was a rumor that Burt the chief of police was secretly an ordained minister.

Now all he needed was the ring.

A WEEK LATER, Ivey had avoided it long enough, and now it was time to visit Mom's grave. It must have been hard for Mom to live in wine country, trying to pretend that she was like everyone else and could stop at one or two drinks.

Speculating wouldn't do any good now, because Mom hadn't stopped drinking even after child protective services threatened to take Ivey away. She didn't stop drinking for Aunt Lucy, who didn't understand why Beth couldn't go out drinking Friday night without winding up under the table.

The cemetery where Mom had been buried was on the outskirts of town, ironically on land rumored to have long ago been occupied by a vineyard that had gone out of business. Ivey hadn't been here since the day of the burial.

Along the way, Ivey stopped at a flower stand and bought a dozen gardenias, Mom's favorite flower. Ivey heard a florist say that gardenias were not a good idea in arrangements—they were fragile and required a precise amount of light and cool nights and the leaves turned brown after being touched, making them almost impossible to work with. But maybe Mom should have what she'd wanted in death, even if she couldn't have it in life.

Ivey bent down and replaced the plastic flowers with the gardenias, even if they wouldn't last long in this environment. Kind of like Mom.

Ivey didn't know what to say to a gravestone. Mom wasn't really here, but maybe Ivey could pretend for a minute. Despite the fact that Mom had made life at home a minefield, Ivey didn't blame her anymore. Some people could be as fragile as the gardenias, and couldn't help but make mistakes.

Mom had made a lot of them, but so had Ivey.

She was learning to forgive herself. "Hi, Mom. Sorry it's been so long. I hope you don't mind me asking, but if there's a special place in heaven for babies that were never born would you please find my baby there? Give her a hug from me."

She didn't want to cry, but when a memory of Jeff's warm hand slipping inside hers on the day of Mom's funeral came to mind, tears flooded her view.

She hadn't heard from Jeff in two weeks, and although she tried to tell herself that fourteen days wasn't all that long, every day seemed to be further proof that Jeff couldn't forgive her. Couldn't trust her, and would never get past her betrayal.

But she wasn't going anywhere. Running wouldn't solve anything. If Jeff thought she'd ever give up on him again, he was about to find out different. She'd wait for him, and give him all the time and space he needed. However much time was necessary for him to realize they were meant to be together. She'd be patient this time. Jeff was right in that life sometimes needed a plan.

Or at least a rough draft. Even if she'd always flown by the seat of her pants, like Mom taught her, this time she'd try a plan.

A stop at Mama's Kitchen was precisely what she needed right now to cheer up this melancholy mood, and a double helping of the Knock You Naked Brownies wouldn't hurt. Today of all days she deserved them.

She arrived at Em's in the late afternoon lull before dinner.

"What'll you have, honey? Made some of my pot roast today. Best in a while." Em pulled out her pad.

"I'm having my dessert before dinner today. Life's too short. I want some Knock You Naked Brownies," Ivey said with a sigh.

"Si, are those brownies ready yet?" Em turned to yell.

"No, woman, I said twenty minutes. Hold the phone. There isn't magic in this oven, ya know!" Si shouted back.

"Good Lord that man will be the death of me yet. I told him to put those in two hours ago, as I live and breathe. I'm sorry, dear. Anything else you want now?"

"No thanks, Em. I think I'm going home." Maybe it was a sign from the universe that one more helping of those brownies would turn Ivey into a size eight overnight.

She walked out the door to an unsettling sight. In plain view outside the diner sat Jeff's car, with a huge pink ribbon draped over the hood. The ribbon was large enough to cover the windshield, and it draped down the sides of the front windows.

She didn't think he'd be too thrilled with the idea, even if, like her, he'd grown used to the ribbons. This one was a bit over the top, and Ivey wondered who the joker could be. She turned in circles and didn't see anyone nearby. Maybe she could take it off herself and he wouldn't be the wiser.

Carefully she pulled on the ribbon.

"Hey, what are you doing?"

Ivey startled and turned to see Jeff standing in the shadows, leaning against the wall of the building. "I didn't see you there. I'm only trying to help. Somebody's idea of a joke."

He moved towards her. "Don't take it off."

"Why not?" Her foolish heart beat triple time against her rib cage as he drew closer.

Please calm down. Don't get your hopes up.

"I kind of like it, seeing as I put it there."

"You did?" Ivey's heart did a weird flip when he reached her side.

"What can I say? I wanted to get in on the fun. I hate to tell you this, Little Face, but you're becoming a little predictable."

"Me? What do you mean?"

"Every afternoon around four you're at the diner." He put one hand on top of the hood, effectively blocking her in on one side.

She felt a little bit pinned in, but in a good way. Had he been watching her? "Where did you get a ribbon this large?"

"Special order two days ago. Did you know you can find anything online?"

"Yes, I do." But probably not love. At least not the kind that made you ache.

He grinned. "All right, so I'm still a planner. I can't help that. It's part of who I am, like taking care of people is part of who you are. I wanted a big enough ribbon so that the whole town could see how crazy I am about you."

Now her heart had entered the Kentucky Derby because he was so close, and she couldn't speak because there was a good possibility she'd been struck mute. Good thing he wasn't touching her, because if he did there was a good chance her knees might give out on her for good.

"I'm sorry," he said, and she thought she might have heard wrong.

"*You're* sorry?" she finally managed to say.

"I'm sorry if I ever made you feel like anything was more important than you are."

Ivey swallowed. She'd heard wrong, somehow, otherwise how could he say exactly what she needed to hear?

His finger traced the curve of her lips. "I love you, Ivey. I want to spend the rest of my life proving that you come first with me."

She was dreaming again. This couldn't be real, because it was too good. Too perfect. When Ivey noticed Em and Si walk outside the diner, and then noticed Ophelia and Genevieve, as well as many other patrons and customers, she had to admit this was no dream. It was her reality, and far better than fiction.

"What's all this?" Ivey glanced in the direction of their audience, who had formed a semi-circle around them.

Jeff reached inside the front pocket of his slacks. "I thought I could use a little support."

He got down on his knees in front of the mini-crowd. She almost gasped because those were a new-looking pair of slacks, and he was kneeling in a parking lot. Had he thought this all the way through, or was he trying unpredictability on for size?

"Marry me, Ivey. Say my timing is right this time. I'm not going to lose another chance with you." He had a beautiful antique-looking ring in his hand.

Ivey's heart broke open, and a zillion tiny butterflies made their way up her stomach and out her throat. "Yes! Of course, yes!"

Was that loud enough? God, she hoped so. She hoped people in the next town heard her loud and clear. Her finger shook as Jeff placed the ring on it.

She tugged Jeff up off his knees and threw her arms around his neck. He pulled her up onto her toes and kissed her square on the lips, deepening the kiss like there was no one else in the lot. No one else in the world. People were clapping, possibly, the sound fading in the background.

Sophia was right behind Jeff then, trying to aim her smart phone over his head. "I can't reach, can you get out of my way?"

"No," Jeff said, kissing Ivey again.

"Well damn, how can I get a selfie with both of you in it?" Sophia complained. "My followers are going to want to see this."

Ivey was vaguely aware of someone, possibly Em, dragging Sophia away, muttering a few expletives. It didn't matter, because she wasn't aware of anything other than the pounding of Jeff's heart beat under her hands.

"Let's celebrate, everyone. Knock You Naked brownies on the house!" Em cried out, and Si groaned.

"Should we go inside?" Ivey asked Jeff.

"No. I'm going to knock you naked," Jeff said, smiling against her mouth.

All things considered, that was a much better offer. She did love her chocolate, but she also wasn't crazy.

"See you later, Em! Thanks anyway," Ivey called out.

Jeff was still holding onto her like he thought if he let go she might disappear. But she wasn't going anywhere. Ever again.

"One more thing. I decided to change specialties, so you're going to be the wife of a resident for a while. I don't know exactly what lies ahead, but I hope you'll be there with me."

"It sounds like an adventure."

They drove home in Jeff's car, but first they took the ribbon off.

ABOUT THE AUTHOR

Heatherly Bell is the bestselling author of over sixty titles under two different pen names. She lives for coffee, craves cupcakes, and occasionally wears real pants.

She lives in Northern California with her family, is all over social media, and loves to hear from readers.

You may reach her at heatherly@ heatherlybell.com

ALSO BY HEATHERLY BELL

LUCKY COWBOY

NASHVILLE COWBOY

BUILT LIKE A COWBOY

COWBOY, IT'S CHRISTMAS

MR. COWBOY

SOLDIER COWBOY

WINNING MR. CHARMING

THE CHARMING CHECKLIST

A CHARMING CHRISTMAS ARRANGEMENT

A CHARMING SINGLE DAD

A CHARMING DOORSTEP BABY

ONCE UPON A CHARMING BOOKSHOP

COMING SOON:

HER FAKE BOYFRIEND

For a complete book catalog, please visit the author's website.

www.ingramcontent.com/pod-product-compliance
Lightning Source LLC
Chambersburg PA
CBHW021156010826
48971CB00014B/2192